The Stunt

D0920673

Nancy Rue

BETHANY HOUSE PUBLISHERS
MINNEAPOLIS, MINNESOTA 55438

This author is represented by the literary agency of Alive Communications, 1465 Kelly Johnson Blvd., Suite 320, Colorado Springs, CO 80920.

A Focus on the Family book
Published by Bethany House Publishers
A Ministry of Bethany Fellowship International
11400 Hampshire Avenue South
Minneapolis, Minnesota 55438
www.bethanyhouse.com

Printed in the United States of America by
Bethany Press International, Minneapolis, Minnesota 55438

Library of Congress Cataloging-in-Publication Data

Rue, Nancy.
    The stunt / Nancy Rue.
        p.   cm. — (Christian heritage series. The Chicago years ; 4)
    Summary: Living in Chicago in 1929, twelve-year-old Rudy takes a stand when a black member of his extended family experiences discrimination and Great-Aunt Gussie leads a workers' rights rally.
    ISBN 1–56179–833–9
    [1. Discrimination Fiction. 2. Prejudices Fiction. 3. Race relations Fiction. 4. Afro-Americans Fiction. 5. Labor movement Fiction. 6. Chicago (Ill.) Fiction. 7. Christian life Fiction.] I. Title. II. Series: Rue, Nancy. Christian heritage series. Chicago years ; 4.
PZ7.R88513St 1999
[Fic]—dc21   99–30013
                                              CIP

99 00 01 02 03 04 05 / 15 14 13 12 11 10 9 8 7 6 5 4 3 2 1

For the "Rue Crue"

Chapter One

*R*udolph, is that a frankfurter I see coming out of your ear?"

"Yes, Aunt Gussie."

Rudy Hutchinson nodded absently and gave his one hundredth bored sigh of the afternoon.

His twin sister, Hildy Helen, poked him in the side. "You just told Aunt Gussie you had a frankfurter in your ear!" she said.

"I wish you did," Little Al said. "I'd eat it. I'm starvin', Miss Gustavio! When are we gonna eat, anyway?"

Aunt Gussie stopped dead on the sidewalk she'd been leading them down and surveyed the three of them from under the narrow brim of her gray cloche hat. Her small, sharp eyes had their usual no-nonsense glitter.

"I am attempting to enlighten you children regarding something important from your past. But you, Alonzo, are thinking about food. You, Hildy Helen, have talked of nothing but your new bathing suit. And you, Rudolph, are daydreaming about heaven knows what." She shifted her weight on her walking stick and shook her head, not a single wave of her gray hair moving. "Eleven years old, and you are all practically hopeless," she said.

"We are, Aunt Gussie," Rudy said. "Don't waste your time on us."

"Yeah, we oughta just skip the history lesson and get to the beach, is what I say." Little Al gave Aunt Gussie one of his Italian charmer grins. "We don't want them new bathing outfits to go to waste."

"You can just stop it, all of you," Aunt Gussie said calmly. "We are going to Haymarket, and we are going to see the monument, and I am going give you a lesson on it—"

"And we are going to enjoy it," Rudy said, "whether we want to or not."

"Precisely, Rudolph." Aunt Gussie stuck her walking stick firmly onto the sidewalk and pointed her nose down Randolph Street. "Now let us get on with it," she said.

"Let's get a wiggle on," Hildy Helen said.

As Aunt Gussie pursed her lips in disapproval, Hildy grinned at Rudy. Aunt Gussie hated for them to use slang, which was exactly why they did it at times like this—when Aunt Gussie was making them do something they didn't want to do. Hildy Helen and Rudy had long since agreed that there was no use fighting their great-aunt when she had her mind made up. But it was more fun if they could at least get her hackles up a little in the process.

Little Al didn't usually join in. Aunt Gussie had rescued Alonzo Delgado from having to do a stint in prison at age 10, and Al knew he had to "keep his nose clean" if he wanted to continue to live with her, the Hutchinson twins, and their father in the big house on Prairie Avenue. So when Hildy Helen and Rudy were complaining, Little Al usually slapped on a charmer smile and went along with whatever Aunt Gussie wanted.

Now seemed to be one of those times. He fell into step beside Aunt Gussie, who since her stroke had slowed down considerably from her former businesslike march, and he chattered on about the new daffodils and the smell of spring air and a number of other things Rudy knew Little Al couldn't have cared a fig about.

Hildy Helen and Rudy followed, dragging their respective high-topped shoes on the sidewalk.

"Where are we going again?" Rudy said to her.

Hildy Helen cocked her head so that her thick dark bob of hair splashed against her cheek. "You really were off in dreamland somewhere," she said. Her brown eyes sparkled. "How much are you going to pay me to tell you so you won't get in trouble with Aunt Gussie?"

"Nothing!"

"Fine, spend the afternoon on the picnic blanket with Aunt Gussie while Al and I go swimming."

Rudy's brow furrowed under the clump of dark curls that always hung over his forehead. He poked his glasses up on his nose with one finger. "All right—I'll do your long division homework for you tonight."

"Applesauce!" Hildy Helen said. "You know I can divide rings around you!"

"Cannot."

"Can, too." Her bow of a mouth made a cute knot. "Tell you what you can do for me, though."

"What?" Rudy said. He felt his eyes narrowing.

"You can let me sit by the window when we take our plane trip to Virginia."

"Says you!" Rudy declared. His eyebrows dipped almost over his brown eyes. "I got dibs on that! I've had 'em for a month!"

"I know, so don't get your knickers in a knot. I'm just razzing you. I don't want the window."

Rudy gave her another glare before he jammed his hands in the pockets of the knickers in question. If there was one thing he was excited about these days, it was the upcoming ride in an actual airplane, all the way to Virginia. He cared as much about the family reunion they were going to as Little Al did about daffodils, but the fact that they were going to fly on a plane was keeping him up nights thinking about it—when he wasn't dreaming about it.

"All right, so I'll tell you for free," Hildy Helen said. "It wouldn't be any fun swimming without you anyway."

Rudy glanced warily at his aunt's back and nodded. "Make it snappy, Hildy. She's probably gonna give us a quiz when we get there or somethin'."

"Well," Hildy said, "this is May the first."

"Jeepers, no kidding?"

"Don't give me the business, or I won't tell you at all!"

"Sorry, go ahead."

"May 1 is a day socialists always celebrate."

"Socialists? Where are *they* from?"

"I don't know where they're from! What kind of question is that?"

"Italians are from Italy. Chinese are from China—"

"They're not from a country, silly. They're some kind of political thing."

"Yuck!" Rudy said. Leave it to Aunt Gussie to be doing something political. He actually liked a lot of things about his aunt, but her love for politics wasn't one of them.

"They're supposed to believe in equal rights for the working people, that's what Aunt Gussie said," Hildy Helen went on. "So on May Day they celebrate workers. Aunt Gussie says we're learning about them today."

"By going to look at some stupid monument?"

"Yeah, it was put there for some people who were killed."

"Some workers?"

"No, some policemen."

"What?"

"That's what she said. There was some kind of riot, and a bunch of people died."

"When was this?" Rudy said.

"1886."

"Then who cares?" Rudy cried. "This is 1929!"

"Aunt Gussie cares," Hildy Helen said, "and you'd better too, or we'll never get to the beach for our picnic. We've teased her enough for today. Just stand there and nod your head and say, 'Oh, how interesting,' and it'll be over with."

Rudy squinted his eyes at her from behind his glasses. "Says you," he said. "Maybe you can do that, but she'd never believe me if I did."

"Just no tricks and fooling around, then," Hildy Helen said. "This is going to be our first trip to the beach this year, and if you mess it up for us, I'll—"

"You'll what?"

"I'll tell Aunt Gussie you tried to teach her parrot to say, 'So's your old man.' "

"Sure, and then I'll tell her that you tasted her goldfish wafers to see if they tasted like the communion crackers at church."

"You would not either!"

Rudy grinned slowly at her, and he could see in her eyes that she knew he would in a heartbeat.

"Just don't spoil it, Rudy," she said.

Rudy straightened his shoulders. "I don't see what you're worried about. I haven't played a joke on anybody or messed anything up in a long time."

"Yeah, but I know how much you hate Aunt Gussie's history lessons," Hildy Helen said. "If anything could tempt you, it would be having to stand there and listen to her talk about something that happened a million years ago."

Rudy just grunted. She was right, of course. During anything else Aunt Gussie dragged them through—operas, ballets, news programs on the radio—Rudy could just drift off and draw pictures in his mind of things like airplanes. But dates and names and old-fashioned junk—how could you draw pictures with that going on?

"Rudy—look out!" Hildy Helen burst out.

Rudy stopped just short of walking up the back of Aunt Gussie's legs. She'd stopped in front of him and was already pointing her walking stick.

"There it is, children," she said.

Rudy looked up. "It" was a bronze sculpture of a policeman. Hildy Helen had been right about that. But he didn't look like Officer O'Dell or Detective Zorn or any of the other officers Rudy had met. This fellow was wearing a long frock coat and had a mustache that made him look as if he'd just stepped off the page of their history textbook. Rudy frowned.

"So what's he famous for?" Little Al said.

"He himself isn't famous for anything," Aunt Gussie said as she gazed reverently at the statue. "It's what he represents that we need to remember."

Hildy gave Rudy a jab in the rib. "Pay attention," she whispered.

"I'm going to tell you children what happened here in Haymarket Square one night 43 years ago," Aunt Gussie said. "It's very important, so I suggest you keep your ears open."

"Because there's going to be a test," Rudy muttered.

Hildy Helen gave him a harder poke this time.

Aunt Gussie situated herself over her walking stick and began. Little Al listened with his eyes bugging out, no doubt to give the impression that he wasn't missing a word. Hildy Helen cocked her head to the side, her usual pose when she was trying to make Aunt Gussie think she was eating it up. Rudy sighed and tried not to doze off.

"Now, then," Aunt Gussie said. "Conditions for the working person in 1886 were dreadful. People were working long hours of drudgery for very little pay. I could tell you stories that would curl your hair."

"Mine's already curly," Rudy said.

Hildy Helen shot him a warning look. Little Al smiled at Aunt Gussie and said, "Tell us some, Miss Gustavio!"

"I think you get the idea," Aunt Gussie said dryly. As charming as Little Al was, she was seldom fooled by him—or by anybody else, for that matter.

"There was a group of people called the International Working People's Association—the IWPA—who were trying to change the situation. It seemed to them that the only people who enjoyed the fruits of the working people's labors were the owners, not the workers themselves."

"No fair!" Little Al said.

Rudy rolled his eyes. Al sure could perform.

"It was grossly unfair," Aunt Gussie said. "The IWPA urged workers to band together and form unions, and if their requests weren't granted, they were encouraged to strike."

"That's the ticket!" Little Al said. "Just haul off and slug those owners, right in the chops!"

"Not that kind of strike, Alonzo," Aunt Gussie said. "To strike in the labor world means to refuse to work."

"I like that!" Rudy said, brightening. "Can we strike in school?"

"No, you cannot," Aunt Gussie said, not moving so much as an eyebrow. "Now, the workers at the McCormick Harvester Works on the South Side, where they manufactured large farming equipment, were on strike. There was trouble at the factory during the strike, smashing of windows and so forth. No one was hurt—until two hundred policemen came on the scene and began swinging their nightsticks and firing their pistols."

"The coppers done that?" Little Al said indignantly.

Aunt Gussie nodded. "Later that night, a workers' newspaper

announced that there was going to be a mass meeting the next night and called on workers to 'destroy the hideous monster that seeks to destroy you!' "

"What did that mean?" Hildy Helen said.

"It meant they wanted the workers to take up arms and get revenge."

"For what?" Little Al said.

"Six strikers had been shot and killed in the fray."

Rudy frowned up at the sculpture. "So why is there a statue of a policeman?"

"I'm coming to that," Aunt Gussie said. "There is more to the story."

Rudy tried not to groan. Knowing Aunt Gussie, this could go on until next spring and they would never get to the beach—much less to Virginia on a plane in a few days.

"So did they have their mess meeting?" Hildy Helen said.

"Mass meeting," Aunt Gussie said. "And yes, they did. The leader said the newspaper had misled them—that this was to be a peaceful gathering."

"Peaceful, huh?" Little Al said, looking somewhat disappointed.

"Sounds boring," Rudy said.

"There were speeches," Aunt Gussie said.

"Sounds even more boring."

"You wouldn't have been bored by Samuel Fielden. He was a fiery speaker, that one."

"If you say so," Rudy said.

"I know so," Aunt Gussie said. "I was here."

In spite of himself, Rudy felt his eyebrows go up.

"You were here?" Hildy Helen said.

"You couldn'ta been, Miss Gustavio," Little Al said. "Forty-three years ago, you weren't even born yet!"

"Spare me the flattery, Alonzo," Aunt Gussie said. "I was 10 years old, and I wanted to know everything that was going on. So I talked my older brother Austin—your grandfather—into bringing me." She gazed back up at the statue. "I'll never forget it," she said. "One minute we were listening as Samuel Fielden told us all to take action for our rights as workers, and the next minute there were 176 policemen standing there almost daring us to raise a hand."

"Did you?" Hildy Helen said.

"I bet you did, Miss Gustavio!" Little Al said. "I bet you was pretty fiery yourself in them days."

"I did not," Aunt Gussie said, still gazing at the statue. "None of us did. In fact, when it started to rain, we all began to go our separate ways." She shook her head in disgust. "The police captain shouted for us to 'disperse peacefully'—and Samuel Fielden shouted back, 'We are peaceful.' And then, from out of nowhere, a bomb was lobbed into the ranks of the police."

"A bomb?" Hildy Helen said.

Even Rudy felt his eyes popping.

"A bomb," Aunt Gussie said.

"Who threw it?" Little Al said.

"No one knows to this day—except the one who threw it," Aunt Gussie said. "No sooner did it go off than shots were fired, some from the workers, some from the policemen. Fifteen minutes later, it was all over. One policeman and six workers were dead. Two hundred other people were injured."

Rudy adjusted his glasses as he looked up at the statue of the policeman. "I don't get it," he said. "You're on the side of the police? I thought you were for the workers."

"I am on neither side," Aunt Gussie said. "I pay my respects at the statue every year because I don't want to forget the mistakes both sides made."

"Why not?" Rudy said. "What's the good in remembering stuff that happened in the Dark Ages, for Pete's sake?"

"Ru-dee!" Hildy Helen said.

"It's all right, Hildegarde," Aunt Gussie said. "That was precisely the question I was hoping one of you would ask."

Rudy gave Hildy Helen a triumphant sniff. She wrinkled her nose at him.

"And here is your answer, Rudolph," Aunt Gussie said. "Those who do not remember the past are doomed to repeat it."

They all looked at her and blinked. Rudy chomped down on the inside of his mouth so he wouldn't say, "I wasn't planning on throwing any bombs anytime soon anyway." Hildy Helen was right; they'd probably pushed Aunt Gussie far enough. It was time to get to the beach. Besides, there was something creepy about that story.

"Fascinatin', Miss Gustavio," Little Al said.

"Mm-hmmm," Aunt Gussie said. She looked at them slyly from under the brim of her hat. "But I think you are all more interested in the immediate future than in the past. I suppose we ought to get to the beach before the weather changes."

Rudy breathed a sigh of relief. That was the thing about Chicago—spring came in spurts. One minute you could be headed to Lake Michigan for a swim, and the next minute a cold wind could come in and practically blow you away. Today it was warm and sunny—too good to be wasting the day in front of some dumb statue he still didn't understand. He could already picture the sand between his toes, and the cold water of Lake Michigan lapping up over his shoulders.

On the way back to Aunt Gussie's long, black Pierce Arrow, which was parked on Clinton Street, Little Al fell in beside Rudy.

"We're almost in your old neighborhood, huh?" Rudy said.

"Yep. I used to sit on this very wall right here."

Rudy looked at the wall that separated Clinton Street from the train tracks below coming out of nearby Union Station.

"You sat here and ate salami?" Rudy said. He and Al had done that on a few walls in their time.

"Nope, I used to wait for the trains to come by and sometimes I'd jump on top of one and get a ride."

"Nuh-unh!"

"I did, Rudolpho."

"You would have killed yourself. Trains move too fast."

"Not when they're just comin' outta the station like that." Little Al smiled smugly. "I'd jump on and ride 'til I felt 'em pickin' up speed, and then I'd jump off on the side of the road. Simple."

Rudy was glad Aunt Gussie's car was just ahead. He was afraid Little Al might suggest they jump aboard a train right now—and it didn't sound so simple to him.

Rudy could see the white hair of Aunt Gussie's old chauffeur, Sol, above the steering wheel. Sol had suffered a blow to his head several months before, and his memory was only starting to come back. Rudy was glad one of the first things he'd remembered was how to drive the car.

Just then the door on the passenger side flew open. A tall, large-boned black woman stepped out. It was Quintonia, Aunt Gussie's maid. Since the stroke, Aunt Gussie seldom went anywhere without her.

"You stood out there way too long, Miss Gustavia," Quintonia said, shaking her head. "You gonna tire yourself out." She glared at the children as if they had dragged their aunt bodily to the statue. "I don't think you oughta be goin' to no beach today."

Before the children could protest, Aunt Gussie put up her hand. "I'm fine, Quintonia," she said. "Some sunshine and fresh air is exactly what we all need."

"And food," Little Al said, bestowing one of his dazzler smiles on Quintonia. "You got that picnic basket full?"

That was a ridiculous question, Rudy thought. Quintonia never let an hour go by without offering something delectable from her kitchen. Rudy knew for a fact there were at least two pies in the basket at that very moment.

But at that very moment, neither he nor Hildy Helen cared about food. The minute Sol parked the Pierce Arrow on 29th Street, the twins were out its back door, hauling down the sidewalk with Little Al hot on their heels.

"Don't you get them shoes wet!" Quintonia shouted after them.

There was no danger of that. Rudy was only too glad to pull his sweaty feet out of his high tops and shed the long socks as well. All three of them left shoes, stockings and clothes in a heap on the sand and tore toward the water in the knit bathing suits they'd been wearing underneath. Little Al and Rudy plunged into Lake Michigan, gasping and shivering. Hildy Helen stopped on shore to tug her red and white striped top over her hips and pull the legs of the red pants to her knees.

"You comin' in?" Little Al shouted to her. "Or do we hafta drag you in?"

"You two and who else?" Hildy Helen said. Then she tossed back her bob and came straight at them, arms flailing.

"Look out! She's gonna splash!" Rudy cried.

He dove underwater and felt it deliciously take his breath away. *Finally, some fun!* he thought.

Hildy Helen was still splashing when she surfaced, which meant he had to dunk her, which led to a splash-and-dunk fest that had them shrieking like the gulls circling over their heads. Rudy was taking Hildy Helen down for the third time in a row when Little Al said, "Hey, what's with the coppers?"

Rudy let go of his sister and held her at arm's length as he squinted up at the shore. Without his glasses it was harder to see, but there was definitely a police officer there. He appeared to be marching straight toward Quintonia, who was setting up Aunt Gussie's deck chair on the sand. There was something about the straightness of his back and the sudden slump in Quintonia's when she saw him that started Rudy's stomach churning.

"Let's go see," Hildy Helen said. "Come on."

They splashed their way out of the water and arrived next to Quintonia just as the police officer did. The three kids stood in a dripping line as the policeman hooked his thumbs into the belt of his jacket and drove his eyes into Quintonia.

"You planning on staying here?" he said.

"Yes sir," she said. "I'm settin' up this here chair for Miss Gustavia Nitz."

She nodded toward Aunt Gussie, who was leaning on Sol's arm and picking her way toward them through the sand. Rudy snickered to himself. It was hard to tell who was helping whom.

But the snicker died in his throat at the police officer's next words.

"She can sit here," he said. "But you can't." He lifted his chin. "This beach is for whites only."

"What's the trouble, officer?" Aunt Gussie said from several feet away.

"No trouble—as long as your mammy here waits for you in the car or takes herself to the Negro beach that's down on 25th Street."

"I'm well aware of where it is," Aunt Gussie said. She stopped at the edge of the blanket and let go of Sol's arm to lean on her walking stick. She was half out of breath, but her voice still sounded strong—the kind of strong that always made Rudy's stomach turn over. He glanced warily at Hildy Helen, but she had her eyes glued to Aunt Gussie.

"Good," the policeman said. "Then you can direct her there."

"I'll do nothing of the kind," Aunt Gussie replied. "Quintonia Hutchinson lives in my home and has ever since I can remember. She goes where I go."

"Well, she can't go here." The policeman's face tightened. "I don't want any trouble here. You didn't witness the race riots that started right here on this beach ten years ago. I did."

"So did I," said Aunt Gussie.

Rudy tried not to roll his eyes. Was there any historical event Aunt Gussie hadn't been to?

"I don't want that repeated," the policeman said.

Rudy could see the muscles on his face twitching. Aunt Gussie's, on the other hand, were perfectly still.

"Nor do I," Aunt Gussie said. "And they won't be if you go on about your business and we go on about ours."

The policeman drew himself up so abruptly, Hildy Helen grabbed onto Rudy's shoulders.

"Are you disobeying an officer's orders?" he said.

"No, I am merely trying to reason with one," Aunt Gussie said. She gave him a hard smile. "But I can see it's pointless. Clearly I am not dealing with a man of conscience."

The policeman looked like a cash register adding up her words.

"You need any help, officer?"

Rudy turned to see that behind them a small crowd had gathered. A man with a large belly and hairy arms stepped forward and was already rolling up his sleeves.

"What's he going to do, punch out Aunt Gussie?" Hildy Helen whispered.

Rudy didn't answer. He just wanted to get away from here.

As if she had read Rudy's mind, Aunt Gussie turned from the stunned face of the police officer and said, "Come along, children, Quintonia, Sol. I have no desire to remain anyplace where members of my family are not welcome."

With a thump of her walking stick, she started back up the beach. Rudy was the first to follow. He felt like the Chicago spring. One minute he couldn't have been torn away from the beach, and the next minute he wanted to get as far away from it as he could.

Chapter Two

*T*he twins' father, Jim Hutchinson, didn't get home until after supper that night, but that wasn't unusual. He worked as a pro bono lawyer—which meant he represented needy clients for free. Sometimes he got so involved in his cases that he forgot to eat.

When he finally appeared, the children and Aunt Gussie were gathered in the library with Aunt Gussie's personal secretary, Bridget McBrien. While Aunt Gussie and redheaded Bridget got ready for a meeting, the kids were pretending to do their homework. Rudy was drawing the officer at the beach, only he was a statue with his arm pointing and his face scowling. Sometimes Rudy used drawing as a way to pray—showing what Jesus might do in a situation—but he wasn't sure how to fit Jesus in with what had happened at the beach.

Picasso, Aunt Gussie's parrot, suddenly announced their father's arrival, shrieking, "Dad! Dad!"

Little Al greeted him with, "A copper give us the bum's rush at the beach today, Mr. Hutchie!"

The vague, I'm-still-at-my-office look in Dad's eyes disappeared instantly as his eyebrows arched over the gold rims of his glasses.

"What's this?" he said.

"Thank you, Alonzo," Aunt Gussie said dryly. "I had planned to let the poor man have his supper and get a look at the newspaper before I sprung that on him."

Quintonia marched in carrying a plate piled with pork chops and French fried potatoes and set it down on the table, but Dad ignored it.

"Go ahead and spring it, Auntie," he said. He squinted at Hildy Helen, then at Little Al, and finally at Rudy. "You three didn't embarrass your aunt at the beach, did you?"

No! Rudy thought. *She embarrassed us!*

But he still wasn't sure exactly why he'd wanted to crawl in a hole when Aunt Gussie had stood up for Quintonia. She was always for the underdog, and she and Dad had both taught the kids to be that way, too.

Besides, he didn't want to get his father frowning at him. He and Dad had actually started getting along better since they'd moved to Chicago, and that was one thing he didn't want to mess up.

"We didn't do nothin', Mr. Hutchie!" Little Al said. "It was that copper done it. I'd a slugged him, only I knew you wouldn't like that."

"Thank you, Al," Dad said, "but does someone want to tell me what the poor officer did to deserve the wrath of Delgado?"

All three kids opened their mouths, but Aunt Gussie put up her hand to silence them. She gave a quick account of what had happened at the beach. Once again, Rudy could feel his face going red when she got to the part where the crowd gathered and everybody was staring at them.

When Aunt Gussie was finished—and Little Al had muttered to Hildy Helen and Rudy that he could have told it a whole lot better—Dad sank into one of the leather chairs and shook his head.

"It doesn't really surprise you, does it, Auntie?" Dad said. "That's the way our society has become, suspicious of anyone who has a drop of foreign blood or skin a shade darker than ghostly white."

"They don't got no reason to be scared of me, Mr. James," Quintonia said. She pushed the plate an inch closer to Dad. "I wish Miss Gustavia hadn't made such a fuss."

Yeah! Rudy thought. *Me, too.* He squirmed in his chair and pondered shooting a spitball at Picasso, just to bring this conversation to an end.

"Be glad she did," Dad said. "That's the only way we're ever going to change things. Right, Rudy?"

Rudy jumped. "Sure, Dad," he said. "I guess so."

"You should know so. After your experiences with Little Al—and then with Isabel—you know, your Jewish friend—you children know we have to stand up for people who are being unjustly persecuted and discriminated against."

"Wooh!" Quintonia said, fanning herself with her hand. "You talkin' lawyer talk now, Mr. James. I don't know them big words."

"Translate for Quintonia, Rudy," Dad said. He put his hand on Rudy's shoulder.

"Uh—" Rudy said. "Uh—we oughta treat everybody the same and respect people even when their ideas are different . . . or something."

"We try to see that everyone gets justice."

"Loving our neighbors as ourselves," Aunt Gussie put in.

Yeah, Rudy thought. *Except when it embarrasses the life outa ya!"*

Quintonia shrugged. "Too bad everybody don't think like you do," she told Dad. "I'll go get your newspaper."

She left, and Dad gave Rudy's shoulder a pat. "You're a man of principle," he said. "Unfortunately, we men of principle are at odds with the times."

"What does that mean?" Hildy Helen said.

There was one more pat as Dad pulled his hand away. "Most of America can be divided into two groups," he said.

Thanks, Hildy Helen, Rudy thought. *Once you get Dad talking about this kind of stuff, it could go on for days.*

"There are those who are frightened to death of anything 'different.' They think Quintonia is inferior because she's black. They think Aunt Gussie is a communist because she believes workers deserve decent wages and working conditions."

"They think she's a Red?" Little Al said.

"If Quintonia's black and Aunt Gussie's red," Rudy said, "what color do they think *you* are, Dad?"

"They sure can't call you yellow, Mr. Hutchie!" Little Al said.

"They'd probably call me a 'pinko,' " Dad said, "because I refuse to run the Quintonias off the beach or tell the Germans to go back to their own country, or—"

Quintonia brought the newspaper in and set it next to Dad's plate. Rudy looked at it longingly. He wanted to flip to the comics and read *Krazy Kat* or turn on the radio—anything but talk about this stuff.

"You said there were two groups," Hildy Helen piped up. "What's the other group?"

"The other group isn't scared enough," Dad said. "At least not of the disaster that I fear lies ahead."

"What kinda disaster?" Little Al said.

Here we go with the business about money, Rudy thought dismally.

Dad was always going on about how people were investing stupidly in the stock market, thinking prosperity was going to last forever, and how someday it was all going to come crashing down. Rudy gave the newspaper a long, wistful look.

"I'm glad the working man can possibly make a fortune," Dad said. "But the economy can't be allowed to run wild."

"Don't forget the working *woman*," Aunt Gussie said briskly. "Speaking of which, Bridget, we're going to be late if we don't leave now."

"I'll tell Sol to bring the car around," Bridget said. She shook out her bob of red curls and stretched behind her desk. Rudy decided she looked as bored as he felt.

"Where are you off to tonight, Miss Gustavia?" Quintonia said, disapproval etched on her lips.

"There's a mass meeting at the garment factory," Aunt Gussie said. "I'm going to encourage the female workers to join the union and perhaps improve their lot."

"You haven't even had your rest today," Quintonia said. "I don't like you goin' out in the night air, carryin' signs with a bunch of people."

"Quintonia," Aunt Gussie said as she reached for her hat, "most of the women I'm going to be speaking to tonight have probably forgotten what rest is."

Quintonia left the library muttering and shaking her head. Picasso mimicked her with a mumbling, "If you catch your death of pneumonia, don't come cryin' to me."

"Any other news today, Auntie?" Dad said, finally reaching for the newspaper. Rudy started to ask for the comics, but Aunt Gussie stopped midway to the door.

"I'm still waiting to hear from Jubilee," she said. "I need her to tell me whether she's going to come here and fly with us to Virginia."

"That's only a few days away, isn't it?" Dad said.

Two days and ten hours, Rudy thought, sitting up straighter in the chair. Now this was a subject he wanted to talk about.

"Somebody's name is Jubilee?" Hildy Helen said. She wrinkled her nose. "And I thought Hildegarde was bad!"

"Careful now," Aunt Gussie said with a twinkle. "Hildegarde has been a good name for me."

"Miss Hildegarde Gustavio!" Little Al said. "It does have a ring to it, Miss Gustavio!"

"No, Alonzo," Aunt Gussie said without looking at him. "You may *not* have a Baby Ruth bar out of the desk drawer. You barely touched your Brussels sprouts at supper." And she sedately left the library with Bridget, cane softly thumping the Oriental rug.

"Your third cousin Charlotte Ravenal named her daughter Jubilee to commemorate the freeing of the slaves," Dad said. "Charlotte was quite a gal. She and my father—your grandfather—were cousins and great friends."

"Dad, can I see the comics, please?" Rudy blurted out. Another second and Dad would be dragging them all down memory lane. He'd had enough history for one day.

"And can I listen to the radio?" Hildy Helen said. "I'll turn it down real low."

"So, this Jubilee doll," Little Al said, "is she a regular dame, or do we gotta mind our Ps and Qs around her?"

"She's very sweet," Dad said, already thumbing through the newspaper, while Hildy Helen dove for the radio with its peacock-fan speakers and Rudy opened up the comics to *Krazy Kat*. "I hope she can make it. She's always had Quintonia's brother, Maxfield, with her and his wife—I forget her name. Anyway, Maxfield died last year and now the wife's ailing, which means Jubilee's taking care of her." Dad paused for a moment over the front page of the *Chicago Tribune*. "That's the way our family has always been with the Negro members of our clan. It would never occur to us to treat them any other way."

"Uh-huh," Rudy said as he turned at last to *Krazy Kat*. Behind him, the radio blared forth—so loudly that he barely heard the doorbell ring.

"Turn that down, Hildy Helen," Dad said, eyes still glued to the *Tribune*.

"It's 'Barney Google,' Dad!" Hildy Helen wailed. "That's my favorite song!"

"I thought 'Ain't We Got Fun?' was your favorite," Little Al said.

"Mr. James, sir?"

It was Quintonia in the doorway, holding a yellow envelope and biting her bottom lip.

"What's the matter?" Dad said. "Who was at the door?"

"Telegram," she said.

She brought it across to him and put it in his hand as if she were handing him a stick of dynamite.

"Telegram?" Little Al said. "Who died?"

"Al!" Hildy Helen said.

"Where I come from, a telegram always means somebody died," Little Al said.

Dad sighed over the opened envelope and nodded. "You're right this time, Al. Somebody did die. Maxfield's wife, Sarah." His eyes got that faraway look again.

"So does that mean that Jubilee person isn't coming?" Rudy said. *Enough with the family history, already!* he thought.

"Oh, she's coming," Dad said. "And she's bringing some people with her."

"Who?" Hildy Helen asked.

"Maxfield and Sarah's two children—that would be your niece and nephew, Quintonia."

Quintonia gave a rare smile. "Little Kenneth and LaDonna!" she said. "I haven't seen LaDonna since she was knee high to a duck. And I haven't laid eyes on Kenneth since the day he was born." Her face suddenly sobered. "You don't think Miss Gustavia will mind, do you, Mr. James?"

"Are you kidding?" Dad said. "These children are family, same as you are. The more the merrier!" His eyes twinkled the way Aunt Gussie's did when she was pleased with the way she was arranging things. "We might have to get a bigger airplane, though, if our party gets much bigger."

That got Rudy's attention. "No, Dad!" he said. "Aunt Gussie said we're going on a Junkers G24! They only hold nine passengers—and they don't make them any bigger. It's the best plane in the air, with three engines—"

Quintonia scowled and jerked her head toward the telegram. "These children just lost their mother, and you still worryin' 'bout your plane ride."

"Now, Quintonia," Dad said, "I'm sure the kids will look after Kenneth and—what was her name?"

Rudy looked quickly at Hildy Helen, and he knew from the way her eyes were going down to slits that she was thinking the same thing he was. Little Al wasn't far behind them. Dad finally went back to his newspaper. Quintonia went out muttering, "If the good Lord meant people to fly, He'da given 'em wings to begin with."

Rudy nodded to the other two, and they met out in the hall.

"You know what this means, don't you?" Hildy Helen said, eyes flashing.

"It doesn't take a professor to figure it out," Rudy said. "Aunt Gussie's gonna expect us to baby-sit those kids."

"You know your onions, Rudolpho," Little Al said. "That's exactly what I was thinkin'." He glowered at the library door. "And I gotta do it, too, or my name's mud with Miss Gustavio."

"Like Rudy and I have a choice either," Hildy Helen said.

Rudy folded his arms and studied the carpet.

"Do you have a plan, Rudy?" Hildy Helen said, voice hopeful.

Rudy shook his head. "Nah. I gotta toe the line, too. I just got Dad to believe I'm not just some goof-up. I think we're stuck."

As soon as he said it, the red-faced, embarrassed feeling welled up in him again. He folded his arms tighter.

"What's wrong?" Hildy Helen said.

"Nothin'," Rudy said.

It was a lie, of course. He just couldn't complain about being stuck with people who were supposed to be family. His father wouldn't like that. Neither would Jesus, that was for sure.

Which made it even worse, because all day he hadn't considered what Jesus would think about anything.

Rudy frowned. "The more the merrier," Dad had said. But was those kids' color going to make it merrier, or messier? Was Aunt Gussie going to make a scene about it wherever they went, like at the beach?

"What is the matter with you, Rudy?" Hildy Helen said. "Your face is turning all red."

"I think I got a sunburn at the beach today," he said.

But he knew it wasn't the sun that was making him burn. He was plain old embarrassed—and something told him there was a lot more of that to come.

Chapter Three

*R*udy got through the next 18 hours or so without blushing. First they went to the Second Presbyterian Church, where he had to keep his mind on the Sunday school lesson and the sermon—since Aunt Gussie always quizzed the children about those at Sunday dinner. He remembered to pray. He drew some sketches on his Sunday school paper of Jesus sitting on the wing of the Junkers G24 while the Hutchinsons all flew inside.

After that, Rudy spent the day at his desk in the room he shared with Little Al, his sketchpad and his airplane books in front of him. He was supposed to be studying for his final examinations, which the children were going to take after they got back from Virginia. But the pictures of Hugo Junkers' planes and the accounts of Charles Lindbergh's flight from New York to Paris called to him a lot louder than his long division problems—and they completely drowned out his history book. Just thinking about George Washington crossing the Delaware in some old, slow-moving boat sent him scrambling for his sketch of the Junkers G24 with its three engines that could cruise at 113 miles an hour.

The only thing that got through was the occasional grunt from Little Al, who was sprawled on the bed reading a primer that was several levels below the one Rudy used. Each grunt was followed by a loud sigh, and punctuated with a hand slapped onto the book. Then there was a louder grunt as Little Al made yet another attempt to get through his assignment.

Finally, Rudy looked up from a diagram of the Junkers engine and said, "What's with you, Little Al? Do you have to go use the washroom or something?"

"I wish that was the problem!" Little Al said. He slammed the book closed and rolled over onto his back. His usually confident little fox face was twisted up. There were tiny beads of sweat on his upper lip.

"What *is* the problem?"

"Readin', writin', and 'rithmetic!"

He picked up the book and hurled it across the room. Rudy watched it smash against the wall and land on the floor.

"You're the smartest kid I know," Rudy said. "Seems like you could learn school stuff all right."

"Well, I can't. I'm gonna flunk all my exams."

Rudy joined him on the bed and flopped down to have his own look at the ceiling. "You haven't flunked any tests all year."

" 'Cause Miss Tibbs always says I started out behind, so she gives me extra points just for tryin'." There was another grunt, this one low and painful sounding. "She told me the other day the principal said she can't do that on the final exams. I have to pass 'em fair and square, or I don't go on to the seventh grade with you 'n' Hildy Helen."

"You will, though," Rudy said. "You'll learn. You're smart enough."

"Says you. But you ain't the teacher, if you know what I mean."

That made for two glum faces when Hildy Helen came in at suppertime and announced that Miss Tibbs was there to join them.

"She's here again?" Rudy said.

"I told you—she and Dad are stuck on each other," Hildy Helen said, adjusting her big, white hair bow in the mirror above the boys' bureau.

"Why can't Dad be stuck on Amelia Earhart?" Rudy said.

"Is *she* a teacher?" Hildy Helen said.

"No, ya stupe! She's the first woman to fly across the Atlantic Ocean."

"In an airplane?"

"Of course in an airplane!" Rudy sputtered. "You think she sprouted wings?"

Hildy Helen sniffed and tossed her bob. "You don't have to get so ugly about it, Rudy. I'm not airplane conscious like you are."

"We're going to fly in one! Don't you want to know all about it?"

"I just want to know we aren't going to crash," Hildy Helen said. She gave a shudder.

"Are you scared to fly?" Little Al said.

"No—well, maybe a little. Aren't you two?"

"Unh-uh," Rudy said. "I can't wait."

"And we can't wait any longer for you in the dining room," said a voice from the doorway.

Rudy grinned at Bridget, but she didn't smile back.

"Are you coming or what?" she said, and disappeared again.

"What's the matter with that doll?" Little Al said.

"I don't know," Hildy Helen said, flouncing toward the door. "It seems like everybody is in a bad mood these days."

That seemed to include Miss Tibbs. Their pretty, blonde, wavy-haired teacher was unusually quiet during supper. She and Dad disappeared behind the closed doors of the library as soon as the apple pie and cheese were cleared away. Little Al, Hildy Helen, and Rudy hung about casually in the front hallway, pretending to read the Sunday paper as they waited for stray words to escape under the door.

"I wish they'd talk louder!" Hildy Helen hissed.

"They're just whisperin' sweet nothings into each other's ears, is what I say," Little Al said.

"Shh!" Hildy Helen said. "I'm trying to listen."

Rudy scanned the book section without interest, although his eyes did catch on a review of a book about George Washington. Was there no getting away from history?

But as he read, he started to grin. Then he chuckled out loud, only to be shushed by Hildy Helen, who pointed at the library door.

Just then the voice of Dad could be heard from within: "That is the most ridiculous thing I have ever heard! And I have heard some ridiculous things, believe me."

"It may be ridiculous, Jim," Rudy heard Miss Tibbs say, "but that's the way it is. I cannot in good conscience pass the boy. He isn't ready to go on to the seventh grade. That's junior high school."

Rudy felt Hildy Helen stiffen beside him. He sneaked a glance at Little Al. He was drilling a hole in the funny papers with his eyes.

"I'm getting pressure from above," Miss Tibbs said. Then her voice trailed off, and Dad's mumbled in reply.

Hildy Helen cleared her throat. "Listen to this," she said, straightening the newspaper. "A woman has been elected governor in Texas! Go, lady!"

"You haven't heard anything!" Rudy chimed in. "Get this. In this book, this fella says George Washington was a great card player and he cursed like a sailor. Wait 'til I tell Miss Tibbs!"

Rudy and Hildy Helen laughed—a little too loud for a little too long. Little Al grinned along with them, but his eyes didn't have their usual spark.

"Hey, and get this!" Hildy Helen went on loudly. "Clarence Tilman, 17, in Warsaw, Indiana, put 40 sticks of chewing gum in his mouth at once, sang 'Home Sweet Home' and, between verses, drank a gallon of milk!"

"Says you!" Rudy cried.

"It's right here in the *Tribune*. It must be true! Don't you think, Al?"

"I don't know!" Little Al cried. He tossed his section of the newspaper away and shot up from the carpet. "I don't know—and I'm never gonna learn!"

He was gone before either of them could say a word.

Hildy Helen sighed as she watched him tear out the front door.

"I was trying to talk loud so he couldn't hear the rest of what Dad and Miss Tibbs were saying," she said.

"Me, too. I don't think it worked."

"You think she was talking about him?" Hildy said.

"Sure she was. What are we gonna do?"

"You got me," Hildy Helen said. "We have those other kids coming that we're supposed to 'look after' and we're going to Virginia soon. When are we gonna have time to get Al ready for exams?"

"We gotta find time," Rudy said. "Who's more important, Little Al or a couple Negro kids we don't even know?"

Hildy Helen gazed off, eyes thoughtful. Rudy was glad she didn't notice his face turning red again.

It was hard to go to school the next day, knowing what Miss Tibbs was going to do with Little Al if they didn't stop her.

"All right, class," she said when they'd done their pledge of allegiance and the school song. "We are going to begin preparing for the history exam today. I'd like to see just how much you remember from what we've learned this year."

Rudy exchanged worried glances with Hildy Helen. Little Al

slumped back in his desk and looked unconcerned.

"I'm going to begin with our study of George Washington," Miss Tibbs said. Her green eyes went straight to Little Al. Rudy caught his breath. "Al?" she said. "What can you tell me about Washington?"

Rudy couldn't look. His own cheeks were already on fire, and he didn't want to see the same shame on his adopted brother's face.

But when he spoke, Little Al's voice was as cocky as usual.

"Well, Miss Dollface," he said. "This may surprise you, but I was just readin' about old George yesterday in the Sunday *Tribune*."

"Oh?" Miss Tibbs said, sandy eyebrows lifting slightly.

"Yeah. Seems like some fella found out somethin' new about him."

"What would that be?"

Rudy looked in time to see Little Al grin. "Seems like he could play cards with the best of 'em—and he was a champion curser. And get this—he could chew 40 sticks of gum at once and drink a gallon of milk!"

The classroom broke into a high-pitched chatter that even Miss Tibbs had to call over to settle down. By then Hildy Helen was sitting with both hands slapped over her mouth, and Rudy was looking at the ceiling, whistling. It didn't fool Miss Tibbs.

"Rudy," she said in her always calm voice. "Why don't you visit with me for a few minutes after school today, hmm?"

"Sure, swell," Rudy said, and gulped.

"And Al," Miss Tibbs said, before she turned to the other side of the room with her list of questions, "I hope that tomorrow you'll be able to tell me some of the more traditional things George Washington is known for."

"Gotcha, Miss Dollface," Little Al said. He was still grinning, but once again the light was missing from his eyes.

Rudy glanced nervously around the room. In the back row, where he always sat with his three nose-picking cohorts, pudgy Maury Worthington drew his finger across his throat. Rudy made a face and turned away. Maury always got a kick out of seeing any of the Hutchinsons get in trouble.

But Maury wasn't too far wrong when he suggested that Rudy was about to get his throat cut. When the school day ended and the rest of the class filed out, leaving Rudy alone with Miss Tibbs, the teacher's green-gold eyes were like daggers.

"I know I have you to thank for Al's somewhat twisted view of American history, Rudy," she said. "And don't deny it, because I heard you spouting that particular piece of misinformation in the hallway at your house yesterday."

All Rudy could do was shrug. He didn't care to talk to her now anyway, not if she was going to flunk a regular fella like his brother.

"That's it?" she said. "That's the only answer you have?"

"I guess," Rudy said. "Except he was wrong about the chewing gum. That was somebody else."

Miss Tibbs fingered a sand-colored curl that rested against her cheek. "This makes me sad," she said. "I thought you and I understood each other better than this."

I thought we did, too. He'd come to like Miss Tibbs, even if she was a teacher, and even if she was "stuck" on his father. She'd stood up for him before. She liked his art. She'd been almost like—a friend.

"What is going on in there?" Miss Tibbs said. She reached out and lightly tapped his forehead.

"I don't know," Rudy said stubbornly.

"First thing that comes into your head," she said.

"All right," Rudy said. "I don't see why Little Al has to know all that history stuff anyway. What good's it ever gonna do him? He's gonna be fine without it!"

She watched him curiously. "Are we talking about Little Al? Or are we talking about you?"

"Me?"

"Yes, you. You know, of course, that whatever is important to you will be important to Al. He looks up to you. He wants to be like you."

"Says you!" Rudy said. He looked down at the desk and said quickly, "Sorry."

"It's as plain as the nose on your face, Rudy. If school were more important to you, it would be more important to Al. You and Hildy and your father and your aunt are the only models he has."

"I do all right in school," Rudy said.

"You do because it comes easily to you. It isn't that way for Little Al. He has to work at it, and he doesn't work at it because you don't."

Rudy shook his head. "Little Al's a tough guy. If he wants to do something, he'll do it, whether I want to or not."

Miss Tibbs sank down into Hildy Helen's empty desk beside Rudy and folded her hands on its top. "You have a right to your own opinion, Rudy," she said, "but this time I want you to think carefully about what I'm saying. You may know Little Al better than I do, but I have something you don't have, and that's experience. I know Little Al is going to respond much more to your attitude than he is to a week's worth of lectures from me." She gave her sure, confident smile. "If you don't believe me, try it yourself."

Rudy didn't answer. He didn't know what he was supposed to say.

"All right, then," Miss Tibbs said. "Let's make a deal. You try showing a better attitude toward, let's say, history, for the week you're gone. If Little Al comes back here and starts to do better, we'll both know I was right and Little Al passes and everyone is happy."

"And if he doesn't?"

"Then you were right," she said. "And we'll all be sad."

Rudy was sad already. His eyes never looked away from the cracks in the sidewalk as he trudged down Prairie Avenue alone, and his thoughts never left Little Al.

She really is gonna flunk him if he doesn't do good on his exams, he thought. *No matter how much he calls her Miss Dollface or how much Dad likes her or anything.*

And he was supposed to help Little Al by doing *what?* Changing how he felt about history and stuff? How could Rudy do that when even the grownups couldn't? He was just a kid, for crying out loud!

He looked up from the sidewalk just in time to see the Pierce Arrow pulling into the driveway at Aunt Gussie's. He could see several heads inside besides Aunt Gussie's and Sol's. Who did they belong to?

He knew as soon as the car stopped and Sol opened the back doors. Out of one stepped a scrawny, tired-looking little black boy of about six whose head appeared to be too big for his thin-limbed body.

From the other door came a young black woman, wearing a pink suit so bright it made Rudy want to shield his eyes. She adjusted her matching hat and smoothed her white-gloved hands down her slim hips as she glared around her. The way her mouth bunched up, it was clear she didn't like what she saw. She leaned over and inspected her hose, which were rolled up just below her knee, and then glowered around her again.

That kid's gotta be Kenneth or whatever his name is, Rudy thought. *And that must be his nanny. I'm sure glad she's not* my *nanny!*

At least there was somebody to baby-sit the kid. Now that he had to make sure Little Al didn't fail the sixth grade, Rudy wasn't going to have time to "look after" Quintonia's relatives.

Just then the front door of the house flew open, and Quintonia burst out, waving her arms and shouting loud enough to be heard all the way to the Loop.

"Kenneth, baby!" she cried. "And LaDonna, is that you? Is that for sure nuff you?" Quintonia bolted for the young woman in the pink suit and crushed her in a hug.

"Yes, I'm LaDonna," the young woman said, standing stiff as a clothesline prop. "Who were you expecting, Raggedy Ann?"

Rudy stopped on the sidewalk and felt his heart sink. Not only wasn't she the kid's nanny, but she was about as nasty-sounding a girl as he'd ever heard. She sounded almost as mean as Maury Worthington.

Aunt Gussie got out of the car with a small, auburn-haired woman that Rudy guessed was "Jubilant" or whatever her name was. Quintonia continued to hug LaDonna and rock her back and forth. Rudy was convinced she was going to stay there forever, but when Quintonia looked over LaDonna's shoulder her eyes snagged Rudy.

"Well, looka here," she said, letting go of her niece. "Just in time! LaDonna, this here is Rudolph. He's your cousin, I reckon, in a way, and he's gonna be your host while you're here."

"Swell," Rudy muttered. And he stepped forward to meet her.

✢·✤·✢

Chapter Four

*H*urry up, now, boy!" Quintonia said. "Don't keep us standing out here in the sun!"

Only because Quintonia was wearing her I'm-not-going-to-
put-up-with-any-nonsense face did Rudy quicken his steps and
walk up to LaDonna. She looked down at him from under the
brim of her pink hat and blinked imperiously. It made Rudy wonder if he were supposed to go down on one knee and kiss her ring.

"H'lo," he said instead.

She put out her hand, and Rudy looked at it blankly. Then he
felt his eyes go wide. This girl had the longest fingernails he'd
ever seen. They were bright pink, and they looked sharp enough
to carve a roast with.

"What are you staring at, boy?" she said. Her voice was sur-
prisingly heavy, considering how skinny she was. Rudy could just
hear Hildy Helen now, raving about how LaDonna had the figure
like a boy that you saw on all the models in the magazines. Rudy
thought she looked kind of like a pole with oiled black waves of
hair on top and rolled-up hose at the bottom.

"I said, what are you staring at?" She clicked her tongue in
disgust and turned to Quintonia. "Is he always this rude, staring
at a person like she was from Mars or something?"

"He hasn't been taught the manners you have," Quintonia said, eyes glinting at Rudy. "But we working on it."

"Looks like you need to work harder," LaDonna said. Then she flicked her face away as if to dismiss Rudy from her audience.

Who do you think you *are?* Rudy thought as she flounced toward the house, heels coming up out of her pink pumps as she walked. *Your shoes don't even fit, and you act like you're some queen—*

Rudy's indignant thoughts trailed off as once more the front door opened and Little Al and Hildy Helen appeared. Rudy figured they'd been watching from the library window to size up LaDonna and her little brother. Rudy wished he'd had that chance. LaDonna's eyes had left him so cold, he hadn't been able to think of a single retort to her remarks.

And she says I'm rude! he thought.

He watched as Hildy Helen and Little Al dutifully shook hands with LaDonna on the front steps. Hildy Helen, of course, launched immediately into raving about LaDonna's pink suit.

"Is it silk?" she said.

"Y'know," Little Al put in, "I like a doll in silk."

LaDonna drew herself up so that she looked to Rudy like a praying mantis about to strike. Thrusting her elbows out, she declared, "Yes, it is silk, naturally. And I don't like being called a doll. I am not someone's plaything."

Little Al continued to grin. "Spunky dame, huh? I like a dame with spunk."

As LaDonna opened her smeared-with-pink-lipstick mouth—probably to protest being called a dame, Rudy decided—Aunt Gussie reached the steps on the arm of the smiling woman with hair the color of an acorn and a turned-up nose.

"Hildegarde, Alonzo," Aunt Gussie said. She swept her eyes around to pull Rudy in. "Rudolph, this is your cousin Jubilee. These are James' twins, and this is my adopted son."

What LaDonna lacked in good nature Jubilee seemed to have. She smiled at them all and laughed a gurgling-brook kind of laugh and didn't pat any heads or pinch any cheeks, for which Rudy was grateful. Meeting LaDonna had put him in an even fouler frame of mind than he'd been when he left school. He wasn't sure he could take any cheek-pinching today.

They gathered in the parlor, and Quintonia rushed into the kitchen and out again with a trayful of lemon ices and shortbread cookies. Rudy sat on the hearth with Little Al and Hildy Helen and kept a wary eye on LaDonna.

She surveyed the tray with her lip bunched up and carefully selected a cookie as if it might be the only one on the plate that wasn't poisoned. She barely missed stabbing herself in the nose with her pink nails as she tasted it.

Kenneth, on the other hand, retreated into Cousin Jubilee's lap and peered out fearfully from under her arm.

"He misses his momma," she whispered.

"We know how that feels, Rudy and me," Hildy Helen said.

"Rudy and I," LaDonna said.

She set the cookie down on her plate. Rudy noticed it was tinged with her pink lipstick. *Yuck*.

"Well, this little trip to Virginia is going to cheer us all up," Jubilee said, her golden-brown eyes shining. "I have no blood ties to the Hutchinson homestead, but I'm so excited about seeing the restoration anyway." She looked at the children perched on the hearth as if they'd just asked for an explanation. "My family's plantation in South Carolina was all but destroyed in the War between the States. That was where my mother, Charlotte, was born, and of course where my mother and your grandfather met when they were about your age." She ran a hand over Kenneth's half-hidden head. "It was also where Quintonia's father, Kenneth and LaDonna's grandfather, was born—"

"As a slave," LaDonna said. She gave a loud sniff and gave Jubilee a chilly look.

"That was a very long time ago," Jubilee said quietly.

"And you will be happy to know, my dear," Aunt Gussie said, "that the plantation we are going to in Yorktown never had slaves—not as long as the Hutchinsons owned it, anyway."

If that was any comfort to LaDonna, she didn't show it. She shrugged and sipped daintily at her lemon ice. Rudy had the urge to slurp noisily at his, just to see her bunch her lip again. He heard Little Al give a soft grunt, and Hildy Helen whispered, "Is she stuck up, or what?"

Before he could answer, the doorbell rang. Rudy jumped to his feet.

"I'll get it, Aunt Gussie," he said. "Seein' how Bridget's not here and Quintonia'll want to tend to her company."

"Lovely boy," he heard Jubilee comment as he fled from the parlor.

Bored boy, Rudy thought. And this was probably only the beginning of the history talk on this trip. Good thing they were flying there on an airplane, or the whole thing would be a week-long, boring lesson.

The doorbell rang again as he crossed the front hall. *Must be some delivery boy in a hurry,* Rudy thought.

But the three figures who faced him when he flung open the door were gray-haired and bespectacled and carried prim purses in their white-gloved hands. Rudy recognized them as some of Aunt Gussie's club women. From the pinched looks on their faces, he was pretty sure they weren't here for a round of bridge.

"Hello, Rudolph," said the lady whose hair was tinged in blue. She was his Sunday school teacher. "Is your Aunt Gustavia in?"

"Certainly she's in," said another woman. She had her glasses on some kind of leash, and they fell to her rather large chest as she brushed past Rudy. "We saw her car parked out front."

The third woman peered around the hall as if she thought Aunt Gussie might be hiding amid the artifacts. Rudy resisted the temptation to fling open the mummy case and shout, "Nope! She's not in there! She must be in the closet!"

"She's in the parlor," he said instead. Before he could announce that she already had company, they practically bowled him over getting past.

I shoulda let Quintonia get it, he thought. *She wouldn't let them push her around.*

He contemplated disappearing upstairs and skipping the rest of this increasingly boring afternoon, but he knew Little Al and Hildy Helen would never forgive him for abandoning them. He followed the three wide, gray-suited forms into the parlor and peeked around them as they stood in the doorway.

Little Al, Hildy Helen, Kenneth, and LaDonna had disappeared, along with Quintonia. Aunt Gussie and Jubilee looked up, smiling. But as soon as Blue Hair spoke, the smiles started to fade.

"Gustavia," Blue Hair said, "I'm sorry that you have company. Perhaps we should talk privately."

"This is my cousin, Mrs. Jubilee—"

"Then you won't mind my speaking candidly in front of her, since she's family."

"Speaking candidly about what?" Aunt Gussie said. The smile was completely gone by now, and her eyebrows had stiffened up. Rudy didn't know what was coming, but whatever it was, it made his stomach churn.

Maybe I will just hightail it upstairs, he thought. *Little Al and Hildy Helen are gone anyway—*

But a clatter from the stairs behind him stopped him before he could even take a step backward. He could hear Hildy Helen saying, "I guess you could share my room, then, if you don't like the third floor."

Her voice stopped as the kids gathered behind him, blocking off his escape. The door from the dining room opened at the same time and Quintonia entered with more cookies. When she saw the club women, her eyes went at once to the floor.

"What is it, Clara?" Aunt Gussie said. "You know I can't abide pussyfooting around. Get to the point."

"Then I will, Gustavia," Miss Glasses-on-a-Leash said. "We've come to warn you about your participation in these workers' marches and meetings you've been going to. Carrying signs and such—"

"I appreciate your concern," Aunt Gussie said, "but they are perfectly safe. This isn't the Haymarket era. There will be no violence. Now why don't you all sit down and have a lemon ice with us and you can hear about Jubilee's trip."

"It is not your safety we are concerned about," said the lady who always seemed to be looking for someone in hiding. Even now she glanced over her shoulder at the children before she continued. "It's your reputation."

"And ours," said Blue Hair.

"What on earth are you talking about?" Aunt Gussie said.

"The unions you are urging these poor women to join! They are evil, Gustavia!"

"Oh, for heaven's sake!"

"They are! You haven't heard about the man who owned the dry cleaning stores? The Master Cleaners and Dyers Association exploded a bomb in his plant because he wouldn't make a donation! All his workers then went on strike. He had to go to Al Capone and pay $25,000 for protection."

"Do you hear yourself, Clara?" Aunt Gussie said. She shook her head at Jubilee. "Isn't it as clear to you as it is to me that it was Al Capone, not the Cleaners and Dyers Association, who was behind the union bombing in the first place?"

Jubilee nodded, and smiled as if she hoped this would be the end of it. But Glasses-on-a-Leash threw her hands in the air.

"This is not about Al Capone! This is about you being labeled a communist."

"And the rest of us with you because we are associated with you," said Clara Blue Hair.

"Miss Gustavio ain't a Red," Little Al whispered behind Rudy.

Rudy just held his breath. Aunt Gussie was drawing herself up on the sofa, which meant an explosion was in their immediate future.

"This has absolutely nothing to do with communism or socialism," she said, voice rising and beginning to crackle. "Al Capone controls 84 unions in this city, and the Master Cleaners and Dyers Association is one of them. Now, I believe that unions in their pure form are a good thing, especially for women workers, and I am going to attempt to keep any more of them from falling into that gangster's hands." She took a breath and went on. "I thought we were all of the same mind when it came to serving our community."

"I will have you know, Gustavia Nitz," said the Look-around Lady, "that I give generously to the Community Chest and three college endowment funds, and I participate every year in the church membership drive."

"Ah, yes," Aunt Gussie said with a sigh. "You're a regular Good Samaritan, Marie."

The Look-around Lady frowned. "I beg your pardon?"

"When is the last time you went out in the streets with the needy?

"Don't look down your nose at us, Gustavia," warned Glasses-on-a-Leash. "We are Christians, too, you know."

"Then why ignore those who work their fingers to the bone and still can't feed their families or keep up their rent?"

There was a great deal of indignant sniffing among the ladies in the doorway—so much that Rudy wanted to pull out his hand-kerchief and pass it around.

"That's tellin' 'em, Miss Gustavio," Little Al whispered.

But Blue Hair wasn't finished. "It certainly isn't my fault those people can't keep food on the table," she said. "My great-uncle, Marshall Field, helped build this city without help from anyone. That is the American way."

"Your great-uncle and Cyrus McCormick and the rest amassed their fortune at the expense of other people!" Aunt Gussie said. She was leaning hard on her walking stick—so hard Rudy thought she'd drive it right through the floor.

"And what about your father-in-law?" said Marie Look-around. She glanced from one wall of the parlor to another. "The man built this house you've lived in ever since you married."

"He went to his grave with a load of guilt," Aunt Gussie said. "And my husband and I spent our entire lives trying to give back what he took away. I am still attempting to do that, and I will thank you not to try to stand in my way."

"It's no use talking to you any longer, then," said Clara Blue Hair. She turned her flabby-cheeked face to the other ladies, who nodded until their own floppy chins jiggled like jam.

"We'll be going," Glasses-on-a-Leash said.

They turned like a regiment of soldiers, nearly running smack into Rudy. Their eyes sprang open when they saw the group behind him.

"You haven't met Quintonia's niece and nephew," Aunt Gussie said. She thumped her walking stick across the room to join them. "This is LaDonna and Kenneth Hutchinson. They've recently lost their mother."

All nodding and sniffing stopped, and Rudy had to look closely to see if the ladies were still breathing. Clara Blue Hair recovered first.

"Will they be staying here with you, Gustavia?" she said.

"Yes," Aunt Gussie said.

"Will they be working for you?"

It was LaDonna's turn to sniff, and she did so loudly. Little Al grinned and Hildy Helen, too, had a gleam in her eyes. But Rudy felt his cheeks start to go red again. Why did everything have to turn into a scene?

"No, they will not," Aunt Gussie said. "They—"

"You know they belong on the South Side," Clara said. "They'll be much happier in their own schools and accommodations."

"Although I don't know where this one is going to find a job," Marie put in, pointing at LaDonna as if she were an item of merchandise on the counter at Marshall Field's. "I suppose she could be useful as a strikebreaker."

"The immigrants get the unskilled positions," said Glasses-on-a-Leash.

"There are several African Methodist Episcopal churches down in the Black Belt," Clara said to LaDonna. "You will be much happier there than at Second Presbyterian—"

"Clara!"

The word came out of Aunt Gussie so sharply that Rudy jumped. He could feel Hildy Helen's fingernails digging into his arm.

"If you must know, LaDonna and Kenneth have come with Jubilee to accompany us to the family reunion on the restored Hutchinson homestead in Yorktown, Virginia. I want all the children to see some portion of their heritage." Aunt Gussie drew a breath that kept all three ladies frozen to their spots. "But if they were going to live here indefinitely, I would still have them here in my home, and I would find a job for LaDonna that was worthy of her talents."

"I see," said Marie coldly. She looked around, this time for the door.

"Well, I don't," Clara said. "What I do see is that you are slowly losing your mind, Gustavia. This nonsense of yours is going to cost you everything you have, you mark my words."

"So marked," Aunt Gussie said mildly. It seemed with that out of her system, she was calm again and wished they would be on their way. Rudy did, too.

"What was that all about?" Jubilee said when Quintonia had shown the ladies to the door while the rest of them gathered in the parlor doorway to watch their exit.

"It was about people who cannot see that discrimination of all kinds must be a thing of the past," Aunt Gussie said. She looked firmly at LaDonna, who stood apart from them with Kenneth clinging to her like a baby koala. "No one in my family will be discriminated against, you can count on that."

Rudy felt the red rising in his cheeks again. If he knew Aunt Gussie, the battle was just beginning.

Chapter Five

*R*udy woke up the next morning, the morning of their trip to Virginia, counting passengers on his fingers for about the hundredth time.

There was Aunt Gussie, Dad, Hildy Helen, himself, Little Al, Quintonia, and Bridget. Jubilee made eight. And they had La-Donna and Kenneth going, which made it ten. The Junkers G24 only carried nine people. It was making his stomach churn.

But if anybody else was worried about it, no one showed it. Quintonia, for instance, was singing in the kitchen as she packed yet another huge picnic basket.

"The plane has 310-horsepower engines," Rudy told her, "but I don't know if it can handle too much excess weight."

"Fine," Quintonia said as she tucked in three more pieces of fried chicken. "I'll just take your portion out. How's that?"

"Never mind," he said.

Dad didn't even go into the office—though Rudy was pretty sure Aunt Gussie had threatened him in some way.

"That's why I've been sending Bridget in there with you all week," Aunt Gussie said to him over a breakfast everyone was too excited to eat. "So you would be all caught up on your work and would have no excuse not to go."

"That's right," Bridget said—though faintly. It was the second time Rudy noticed that she wasn't talking much. Usually the twins and Little Al had to compete with her to get a word in edgewise at the table.

She was no match for them today, though. There were questions flying back and forth over the poached eggs and country ham like excited bees.

"Will we still be able to see the ground from the airplane?" Hildy Helen asked.

"Of course," Rudy said loftily. "The ceiling for the Junkers is only 15,420 feet."

Hildy Helen squeezed her eyes shut and squealed.

"Thank you, Rudy," Dad said, eyes twinkling. "That certainly helped Hildy Helen with her fears."

"There's nothing to be afraid of," Rudy said. "That plane has a range of 808 miles before it has to stop to refuel."

"I have to go 800 miles without touching the ground?" she cried.

"It goes 113 miles an hour!" Rudy said.

"Calculate that for me, Rudolph," Aunt Gussie said, winking at Jubilee. "How long will it take us to get to Richmond, then?"

"Not long enough for me," Rudy said. "I can't wait to fly. I want to stay up there forever!"

"That would suit me just fine."

They all looked at LaDonna, who was watching Rudy disdainfully from over her tumbler of milk. Her fingernails, Rudy noticed, were bright orange today.

"As long as I'm not stuck up there with you," she added.

"LaDonna Hutchinson!" Quintonia said. She put her big hands firmly on her hips. "What kind of talk is that?"

"May I be excused?" LaDonna said instead of answering.

"Certainly, dear," Aunt Gussie said.

LaDonna dabbed at her mouth, leaving a smear of orange lipstick on the linen napkin, and slipped out of the dining room in a flow of yellow silky stuff. Rudy thought she looked like a tall, thin banana in her outfit, but he wasn't going to say so. He might get his throat slit while he was sleeping or something.

"Excuse me, Aunt Gussie," Hildy Helen said, "but if Rudy or I had said something like that, you would have sent us to our rooms for the rest of our lives."

"You'da sent me back to jail," Little Al said.

"I'm giving LaDonna a little leeway," Aunt Gussie said. "The girl's mother just died. This is a difficult time for her."

"I appreciate that, Gussie," Jubilee said. "I was almost at the end of my rope with her before our talk last night."

And I'm gonna be at the end of mine if I have to sit next to her, Rudy thought. He drew his napkin across his mouth and stood up.

"May I be excused, too?" he said.

"You didn't eat hardly anything," Quintonia said, eyeing his plate.

"I'm too excited to eat," Rudy said.

That excitement didn't wane even as Dad, Sol, Rudy and Little Al struggled to fit everyone's luggage into the trunk of the Pierce Arrow.

"You might have to make two trips to the airport, Sol," Dad told him, grinning.

We might have to take two planes, Rudy thought. Again he nervously counted passengers on his fingers and hoped the pilot wouldn't notice that they had 10 people instead of nine.

Finally all 10 of them and Sol were stuffed into the Pierce Arrow and headed through the city toward the Chicago Municipal Airport.

"This airport has 36 scheduled flights arriving and departing daily," Rudy announced.

LaDonna clicked her tongue. "Can't he talk about anything else?" she said to Hildy Helen.

"I don't know," Hildy Helen said, grinning at Rudy. "Let's ask him. Hey, Rudy, can you talk about anything else besides airplanes and airports?"

"A National Air Transport flight from Chicago to New York takes six and a half hours," Rudy said. "Does that answer your question?"

"LaDonna, Kenneth," Jubilee said, "here's your chance to get another look at Chicago."

Kenneth, who was sitting on her lap as usual, buried his face in the front of her traveling suit and gave a whimper. It was the first sound Rudy had heard him make since he'd been there.

LaDonna, on the other hand, immediately turned to the side glass and stared at the city. It was the first interest she'd taken in anything, and Rudy couldn't help following her gaze to see what she was looking at.

Probably, he decided, the same things he had looked at when he'd first arrived in Chicago from Indiana nearly a year ago. He'd been overwhelmed by the breathtakingly tall buildings with all their steel and stone . . . the elevated train, the El, that shook the ground as it clattered overhead . . . the screeching of streetcars, the honking of horns, the crush of many of the city's three million people on the sidewalks in an endless hurry . . .

It had been nerve-rattling for him. It also made him feel lonely. He could only imagine how it must be for LaDonna. She'd just lost her mother, too. For the first time, he felt a little sorry for her.

"You get used to it," he said to her. "This is the Loop we're in now. It looks like there's about a million windows, but they all got real people behind 'em, just like any other place. And those taxi drivers that drive like maniacs? They're all right. They can tell you just about anything you want to know about the city."

She turned her face slowly to him, and there was an unmistakable sneer on her lips. "No kidding?" she said. "I think I'll hail one now and ask him why the little boys in Chicago talk so much."

Then she turned back to the window and resumed her survey of the city.

Fine, Rudy thought. *See if I try to help* you *anymore.*

He concentrated then on the road to the airport, counting every light pole, reading every electric sign with its yellow lights, until finally they were there. Rudy thought he was going to come out of his skin.

"You know so much about planes now, Rudolpho," Little Al said, "I bet you could almost fly it yourself."

"I'm going to pass on that," Bridget said.

Rudy looked at her quickly. At least she was smiling now. She also had Kenneth on her lap. It seemed strange to see Cousin Jubilee without him attached to her like a third arm.

Rudy was smiling himself as he climbed out of the car and itched to race across the tarmac to the waiting plane. There it was, on its assigned spot in this private section of the airport, its sleek wings spread proudly to their full 98-foot span, its three propellers waiting to lose themselves in their spin, its nine windows lined up on the fuselage.

Nine windows. Rudy tried to ignore his churning stomach and jumped up and down, first on one foot, then on the other.

"Go ahead, Rudolph," Aunt Gussie said, "before you burst a blood vessel."

Rudy didn't wait for her to change her mind. He took off across the tarmac at a dead run, hearing Hildy Helen and Little Al behind him. He stopped just short of the set of steps that slanted down from the open doorway and gazed up.

"Jeepers," he whispered, "it's even sweller than the ones in the pictures."

"She's a beauty, all right," someone said. A broad-shouldered man in a leather jacket and tight-fitting cap with its strap swinging below his chin appeared from the other side of the plane and grinned at them.

"Are you the pilot?" Rudy said, barely able to breathe.

"I am. And I assume you three are my passengers."

"We are!" Little Al said. He stuck out his hand and shook the pilot's vigorously. "Rudolpho here, he's my brother. He knows enough about this plane to practically fly it himself."

"No, I don't!" Rudy said.

But the pilot was still smiling. "I don't suppose you'd want a peek at the cockpit, then, would you?" he said.

Rudy couldn't even answer. He just bobbed his head up and down and followed the pilot up the stairs. He stopped for a second just inside, closed his eyes, and inhaled. It was hard to believe he was finally in a plane, after months of reading about them and talking about them and drawing them.

"Pinch me, Hildy," he whispered. She did—hard, of course. At least he knew it wasn't just a dream.

There were nine seats, all with velvety looking covers and little square windows.

"It sure is small," Hildy Helen said. "Are you sure it's safe?"

"Safer than driving the highways in a Model A," the pilot said. "Not as much traffic."

Hildy Helen giggled nervously as they followed the pilot through a tiny doorway. The man had to duck to get through. Before them were three seats, two steering wheels, and a sea of dials and knobs.

"What's all this for?" Little Al said.

"It would take me all day to explain it to you," the pilot said. He winked at Rudy. "Perhaps your brother can fill in the details. Basically, this is how the plane flies."

He slipped into the seat on the left; Rudy immediately went

into dream mode. *I want to do this someday*, he thought. *I want to sit in a seat just like that one and know what every one of those knobs is for.*

Rudy shook his head a little and tried to pay attention to what the pilot was saying. There were a few things he didn't know about the Junkers G24, and he was probably about to find them out.

"To make the plane climb higher," the pilot was saying, "you pull the wheel toward you, like this."

He did, and then he stopped and leaned toward the slanted window in front of him.

"What's this?" he said, almost to himself.

The kids all crowded behind him to look out. udy didn't see anything except the rest of their traveling party approaching the plane. He swallowed hard. *He's already counted,* Rudy thought, *and he knows we have too many people.*

Sure enough, the pilot turned to the kids and said, "Are all those people planning to go on this trip?"

"That's our whole family almost," Little Al said proudly. "I'm adopted, of course, but we're all family—"

"Well, that whole 'family' is not going to fly on this plane," the pilot said. He jerked out of the seat much less gracefully than he had slipped into it and pushed Rudy and Hildy Helen aside to get to the door.

But who's going to get left behind? Rudy thought wildly. *Not me! I've been counting on this for a long time!*

He felt himself going red again, and he hurried out of the cockpit to join Hildy Helen and Little Al in the doorway. The rest of the clan was at the bottom of the steps. The pilot was in between, pointing his finger down at Aunt Gussie.

Bad move, Rudy thought. *You don't point your finger at Aunt Gussie.*

"I know this is a few more than we expected," Aunt Gussie

was saying, putting her hand up to shield her eyes from the sun. "But Kenneth can't weigh 50 pounds. Surely that won't make any difference."

"That's not the problem," the pilot said.

Rudy looked at him sharply. His voice had lost its proud friendliness. It was hard and short now.

"I only need one crew member for this flight," he went on. "Without the third crewman, I can take more passengers."

"Then I don't see what the problem is," Aunt Gussie said.

"Weight's not the problem," the pilot said again.

Then what is *it?* Rudy wanted to scream at him.

"The problem is color." The pilot pointed at Kenneth, who was now cowering behind Bridget's skirt. Then he pointed at LaDonna and finally at Quintonia.

Dad cleared his throat. "Sir, you are not saying that—"

"What I'm saying is—" The pilot gave LaDonna one last hard look. "What I'm saying is I don't take Negroes on my plane. These three can't go."

Chapter Six

F or a wild moment, Rudy had a picture in his mind of Quintonia leading LaDonna and Kenneth back to the Pierce Arrow while the rest of them took flight on the Junkers.

But that picture was quickly replaced by what he should have known would happen.

Aunt Gussie slowly brought her hand down from over her eyes and stared, unblinking, at the pilot.

"Surely you can't be serious, young man," she said.

The pilot stuck out his chin like a defiant little boy. "I'm completely serious," he said.

Rudy's heart began to sink. *Please don't say it, Aunt Gussie. Please, Jesus, don't let her say what I know she's going to say.*

Aunt Gussie looked at Dad. He nodded solemnly. Rudy knew there was no hope now.

"Very well, then, sir," Aunt Gussie said. "If these three cannot fly, then none of us will. We shall find other means of getting to Richmond."

"Good luck, lady," the pilot said. His voice was almost vicious. "But I don't think you'll find a private plane at this airport that'll take spades."

Aunt Gussie had begun to turn away. But at that she stopped

in mid-swivel and thrust her eyes into the young pilot as if they were a pair of swords.

"What did you call my family?" she demanded.

Rudy's cheeks were suddenly on fire. Beside him, Hildy Helen groaned. Only Little Al whispered, "Get 'im, Miss Gustavio. Let 'im have it."

When the pilot didn't answer, Aunt Gussie took a step forward. "You may allow your ridiculous bigotry to interfere with your business, son," she said. "You're only hurting yourself by doing that. But when you sling derogatory names at members of my family, you have me to reckon with."

"And me," Dad said.

"And myself as well," Jubilee put in.

"All right, all right, I take it back," the pilot said tightly. "Now all of you, get off my property."

"Oh, with pleasure," Aunt Gussie said. "With pleasure."

But it was not with pleasure that Rudy dragged himself down the steps of the plane and followed the family back across the tarmac to the waiting Pierce Arrow. This felt like a dream—a nightmare. He wished he'd wake up.

They were all silent as they climbed into the car. Only when Sol looked blankly at Aunt Gussie for directions did Hildy Helen say, "Does this mean we aren't going to Virginia after all?"

"Certainly not. Sol, Union Station. We'll catch the next train to Norfolk. That's even closer than Richmond. We'll be there by morning."

A cheer went up in the car, but Rudy didn't join in. *Goody,* he thought. *A train. I've been on a hundred trains. This'll be about as much fun as a flat tire. Why does Aunt Gussie have to be such a wet blanket?*

Just as the thought went through his mind, Rudy looked up and caught LaDonna staring at him from under the brim of her banana yellow hat. The way she was looking at him, as if she wanted to slap him, he was afraid he'd spoken it out loud.

No one else had heard it if he had. They were all talking in forced, cheerful voices, discussing how much safer trains were anyway.

La Donna clicked her tongue at him and looked away.

What are you mad at me *for?* Rudy thought. You're *the reason we're not in the air right now, not me!*

He felt his face going red again, and he sat back and folded his arms. What did he have to be embarrassed about? All his hopes for this trip had just been smashed. From now on, it was just going to be another history lesson.

"I didn't trust that flyboy anyway," Little Al said. "You sure showed him, Miss Gustavio."

"I'm sorry, Rudy," Hildy Helen whispered. "I know how much you wanted to fly."

Rudy shrugged. There was a lump in his throat, and for sure he didn't want to cry right here in front of everybody. Wouldn't LaDonna have a field day with him boo-hooing all the way to the train station?

Aunt Gussie had them wait on benches in massive Union Station while she and Dad and Jubilee went to see what they could do about tickets to Norfolk.

"No, I want to go with you!" Kenneth wailed when Jubilee put him down on the bench.

"I'll stay with you," Bridget said.

She held out her arms, and Kenneth crawled into them.

I'm sure glad she's here, Rudy thought. *I'd hate to have to baby-sit that whiner on top of everything else.*

"Look around, Kenneth," Hildy Helen said. "Is this about the biggest place you've ever seen?"

LaDonna gave the expected sniff. Those sniffs were starting to go up Rudy's spine like a fingernail on a chalkboard.

"Yeah," he said, his voice edged with sarcasm. "Aren't these the biggest columns you ever saw? I could sit and look at them for at least 10 seconds without getting bored."

"For Pete's sake, Rudy," Hildy Helen said. "I was just trying to cheer the kid up. See those two figures there at the entrance to the passageway, Kenneth?"

The little boy nodded his too-big head.

"Those are Night and Day."

"Wow," Rudy said. He rolled his eyes.

"We all know you're disappointed, Rudy," Hildy Helen said with her hands on her hips. "But you don't have to be so evil about it."

"I don't think the boy knows any other way to be," LaDonna said.

"Says you!" Rudy retorted.

"Lay off, would ya, Rudolpho?" Little Al said.

Rudy looked at him, stung. "Whose side are you on?" he said.

Little Al forced a grin. "I'm always on the side of the dames, if you know what I mean. It's safer that way."

"I don't need you on my side," LaDonna said. "I do quite well on my own, thank you."

"I'm sure you do," Little Al said. "I like a doll like you."

LaDonna didn't bother sniffing. She just stood up and walked over to a large Corinthian column, took a compact out of her yellow purse, and started powdering her nose.

"I sure hope Aunt Gussie doesn't see her using makeup right out here in public," Hildy Helen said.

"I already heard her tell LaDonna not to let the tops of her stockings show like that. She said for her to roll them above her knee."

"I'm with you," Bridget said. "I don't want to be around for this scene. You want to go for a little walk, Kenneth?"

The boy nodded anxiously, and the two of them strolled off. Hildy Helen folded her arms and glared at Rudy.

"What?" he said.

"You are being just . . . mean," she said.

Rudy looked helplessly at Little Al, who only nodded.

"I gotta agree with the doll again this time, Rudolpho," he said. "You gotta treat dames better or they turn on you."

"You're as bad as that stupid pilot," Hildy Helen said.

That set fire to Rudy's face. It was impossible for him to stand there any longer. He shoved his hands into the pockets of his knickers and stomped off to lean against a column.

What is the matter with everybody? he thought miserably. *All we do is argue and get disappointed.*

It made his stomach churn so hard he was sure he was going to get sick. The only thing worse than crying in front of everybody would be throwing up. Something had to be done. The question was, what?

Twisting around the column, he saw that LaDonna was still standing against the next one down, sucking her cheeks in like a fish and applying rouge to her now protruding cheekbones.

She was the one responsible for all this, he told himself again. *Why did she have to show up and spoil the whole trip?* Quintonia would gladly have stayed home with Sol if it had just been her, he was sure of that. And now this LaDonna girl was making him behave like a brat again with all her miserable comments. Even Hildy Helen was mad at him, and that almost never happened. And Little Al. What had happened to his loyalty? This girl was even making him into a turncoat.

With a feeling brewing in his head that he hadn't had in a while, Rudy poked around in there for an idea. He took one more long look at LaDonna, and he found one—right there below her knees.

He glanced longingly at Hildy Helen and Little Al. It would sure be more fun to have them in on this with him—and easier, too. One of them could distract her while he and the other one ran up to her and—

But when Hildy Helen caught him looking at her, she pulled her eyes into slits and turned away. Little Al wouldn't even look at him.

Be that way, Rudy thought. *I'll keep all the fun for myself.*

He snapped his head back toward LaDonna. It was perfect. She had just tucked her rouge back into her handbag and pulled out another mirror which she gazed into, wide-eyed, as she fussed with the oily Marcel waves she had plastered to her forehead beneath the brim of her hat.

Stealthily, Rudy came away from his column and fell into step with a woman passing by with a baby carriage. LaDonna didn't look up as he walked in the wake of the carriage and came to rest on the other side of her column.

He waited a few seconds, just to be sure she hadn't sensed his presence—and that Hildy Helen and Little Al weren't going to give him away. But they all seemed to have lost interest in his whereabouts, which was just the way he wanted it right now.

Slowly, without breathing, Rudy moved ever so slightly around the column so he could get a full picture of LaDonna. She was still doing a microscopic examination of her hair. Careful to do it all in one continuous motion, Rudy slid down the column, reached out with both hands, and yanked LaDonna's rayon stocking down to her right ankle. Before she could even cry out, he did the same to the left one, then jumped back into the flow of bodies moving toward their trains.

LaDonna's screech echoed through the high-ceilinged station, and Rudy clapped his hands over his mouth to keep from guffawing even louder.

He would have liked to look back to see her diving to pull her stockings back up, possibly knocking off that ridiculous banana hat in the process, but he didn't dare chance it. He stayed with the crowd until he came to the men's washroom and slipped into it. He leaned against one of the wash basins to have a good laugh, but nothing would come. He couldn't even smile at himself in the mirror. He only noticed that his cheeks were blotchy red.

Rudy waited until they turned their usual color again and he could at least get a cocky grin going. Then he casually exited the washroom, whistling and walking with his hands in his pockets. He stopped when he caught sight of the bench where he'd left Hildy Helen and Little Al. Everybody was back there, and nobody looked happy.

You can pull this off, Rudy told himself. *Just act normal.* He only wished his cheeks weren't going red again.

But no one seemed to notice when he walked up. Everybody was looking at LaDonna, and Aunt Gussie was holding forth.

"I cannot tell you how sorry I am that you've had to go through all this today, LaDonna," she was saying.

"It's certainly not the kind of welcome I expected from Chicago," LaDonna said. She pulled on the lapels of her yellow jacket as if she expected someone to come along and rip it off her any minute. Rudy wished halfheartedly that he'd thought of that.

"I was told," she went on, "that things were differen here than in the South. I was told that up here a Negro could live with a little less fear. I was told you could sit next to a white person on a streetcar and not be thrown off. And I almost believed it."

She let her restless eyes stop on Rudy, and for an awful moment he was sure she'd seen him pull her stockings down and was going to blow the whistle on him right there. His heart stopped beating.

"When we left Alabama," LaDonna continued, "we had to sit in the Negro car. Correction—I had to stand up. I let Kenneth have the only seat left. And that car was hooked onto the end of the train. You know what that was like."

"Ugh!" Bridget said. She hugged Kenneth tighter to her and

rocked him. "All those fumes and all that dirt! No wonder this little boy is sick!"

"But the minute we crossed the Mason-Dixon line," LaDonna went on, "I said, 'Come on, Kenneth. We're changing cars, and we're going to find the first empty seats next to a white person, and we're going to sit there.'"

"Did you do it?" Hildy Helen said.

"They did!" Jubilee said. Her golden eyes were shining proudly. "Then I found them waiting for me in the dining car. We celebrated as we crossed the Ohio River."

"Even when I saw the filth hanging over this city when we arrived," LaDonna said, "I thought I'd come to paradise."

"That was the factory smoke," Bridget said. "I hate it, too." She hugged Kenneth even tighter, as if to protect him from the gray pall that hung over the mills.

"But it isn't paradise, is it?" LaDonna said.

"No, it isn't," Aunt Gussie said. "I'm sad to say there is prejudice here. It's a little more subtle than it is where you come from, but it's here."

LaDonna, of course, sniffed. "I would rather have it hitting me straight in the face than sneaking up on me from behind. I'm glad I don't have to live here."

I'm glad you don't, too, Rudy thought. At the moment he was feeling immensely relieved. If she had seen him yank down her stockings, she obviously wasn't going to tell. *Victory*, he thought.

But somehow he didn't feel much like celebrating.

"So, did you get us a train?" Bridget said to Aunt Gussie.

"I did—a train with a super-powered steam locomotive. Rudy, that should make you happy, eh?"

Rudy grunted as he followed the group down to the tracks. Even the sight of the big Hudson with its steam pouring out didn't make him happy. The spotlessly uniformed men who directed them aboard with military precision did nothing to improve his mood. And he could barely look at the gang of excited young people standing on the back of the caboose, leaning out and waving enthusiastically to those unlucky enough to be left behind.

But nothing made him as unhappy as the moment just before he climbed aboard. He reached up to pull himself on, when he felt something tug at the back of his jacket. He looked back to see Hildy Helen still on the ground, eyes smoldering.

"What?" Rudy said. "I know you're mad at me, so don't yell at me anymore. I'm sick of it."

"And I'm sick of you, Rudy Hutchinson," she said. "I know it was you."

"You know it was me what?" he said. His mind started to whirl.

"I know it was you pulled LaDonna's stockings down right in the middle of Union Station. I didn't see you, but I know." Her brown eyes narrowed at him. "And I think it's the meanest thing anybody ever thought of! From now on, just don't even talk to me!"

Chapter Seven

*I*t was a lonely ride for Rudy on that train to Norfolk. Everyone else seemed bent on convincing themselves that being on a noisy, rocking train was far more fun than going on an airplane could ever have been.

"There are still some top-of-the-line trains left, I see, Auntie," Dad said as he fingered the plush seat he was sitting in.

"The Twentieth Century Limited is one of the best," Aunt Gussie said.

Little Al grinned at her over the top of a strawberry ice cream. "Yeah, well, this musta cost you some heavy sugar."

"Translation, please."

"Dough. You know, cash."

"Ah, well, I don't mind spending money for something that's worth it."

What's a bunch of steam worth? Rudy thought miserably as he stared at the countryside flashing by outside the window. *This thing pants and clanks and hisses. It's enough to drive you batty.* He tried not to think how lonesome its steam whistle sounded.

It wasn't just the train that was making him feel so alone anyway. It was the way Hildy Helen was avoiding him—the way she was trying to take up with LaDonna.

62

"How do you get your eyebrows so thin?" Rudy heard her ask.

"You sure ask a lot of personal questions," LaDonna said. "If you must know, I tweeze them."

"Doesn't it hurt?" Hildy Helen said.

LaDonna sniffed. Rudy turned back to the window. What he'd done served her right, he decided. Now who was being mean? Couldn't Hildy Helen see that?

Aunt Gussie had managed to arrange for a sleeping car, which they settled into at dark. It would have been fun if anybody had been speaking to him. Even Little Al was cranky as they crawled into an upper berth together.

"You can't have the whole thing to yerself, Rudolpho," he said. "Leave me some room, would ya?"

Rudy flattened himself against the wall and squeezed his eyes shut.

"What's eatin' you, anyway?" Al said.

"I'm sleeping," Rudy said. "Leave me alone."

He secretly hoped Little Al would ignore that like he usually did and poke at him until he answered. But Little Al took him at his word, turned over, and was soon breathing like the locomotive that carried them to Virginia.

They arrived at dawn and stepped off the train, still rubbing their eyes. Rudy didn't ask how they were getting to Yorktown from here. He was afraid no one would tell him.

Besides, the answer appeared the moment Dad helped Aunt Gussie from the train.

A wiry-looking man in a checked suit with shoulder pads nearly as wide as the train tracks leaped out of the crowd and cried, "Gussie! Baby sister!"

"Baby sister?" Hildy Helen murmured beside him.

"Jefferson!" Aunt Gussie said.

She hobbled down the steps and into the arms of the man who kept gurgling, "Baby sister!" over and over.

"Isn't this the most embarrassing scene you ever saw?" someone said at Rudy's elbow.

He looked at LaDonna. Her lipstick-smeared lip was bunched up, and she was observing Aunt Gussie and Jefferson's reunion with rolling eyes.

"It's family," Little Al said. "We Italians, we do that when we haven't seen somebody in an hour!"

LaDonna looked extremely grateful that she wasn't Italian and once again reached into her purse for her powder and mirror. Rudy didn't even think of playing a trick on her this time. He was too busy watching the action on the platform.

Jefferson, who was obviously Aunt Gussie's older brother, had white hair which he wore pomaded flat to his head and parted down the middle. He couldn't have had on a louder necktie. It practically shouted its red and purple leaves across the station. His patent leather shoes were the pointiest on record, Rudy was sure. When Dad stepped up to him, in his cable knit sweater and golfer's beret, he looked like a drawing in black and white next to a wild Picasso oil painting. Rudy sketched it in his mind for later drawing.

"Children," Aunt Gussie called to them, "come meet your Great-uncle Jefferson."

"It's a pleasure," Little Al said to him, poking out his hand.

Uncle Jefferson returned the handshake and grinned at Little Al. His smile, Rudy noted, was impish—like a little boy who was up to no good.

"No, no, the pleasure's all mine," Uncle Jefferson said. "But I have to ask—where did this one come from, Gussie?"

"Little Italy," Little Al said. "Miss Gustavio, she adopted me."

"Did she now?" Uncle Jefferson appraised Little Al and grinned again. "I bet you give her a run for her money, don't you, fella?"

"Me?" Little Al said.

"No one gives Gustavia Nitz a run for anything," Aunt Gussie said. "And don't you forget it."

"As if I could," Uncle Jefferson said. Then he winked at Little Al and turned to Hildy Helen.

"Jimmy Hutchinson," he said, "you could not have sired this beautiful young woman—not a chance."

"She looks like her mother," Dad said.

For an instant, Uncle Jefferson looked sad. Then he brought both of Hildy Helen's hands up to his lips and kissed them. She went crimson, but the way she stared at her palms when he let them go, Rudy was sure she'd refuse to wash them for the rest of the day.

I sure hope he isn't planning to do that to me, he thought.

There wasn't time to run. Uncle Jefferson had already grasped him by the shoulder and was looking at him intently.

"Now here is a Hutchinson," he said. "Look at those eyes."

Rudy fumbled. "I thought most of the Hutchinsons had blue eyes."

"I'm not talking about the color—no, no, no," Jefferson said. "No, it's the intensity. You see it, don't you, Gussie?"

"I see it," Aunt Gussie said.

"Your Grandfather Austin had it," Jefferson said to Rudy. "Your Great-grandfather Wesley had it. Your father and your Aunt Gussie here have it." He squeezed Rudy's shoulder. "I pity you, boy. Great things are going to be expected of you. Those of us without that God-given spark can get away with being actors and such. But you, you're going to have to follow in their footsteps."

Rudy tried to smile, but he felt queasy. All this talk about doing great things made him nervous.

The "remember when" talk continued as the now even larger clan of Hutchinsons climbed into cars. Little Al and Hildy Helen begged to ride with Uncle Jefferson in his teal-blue Dusenberg with its white top and its chrome winking in the sun. But Rudy piled in with the rest in one of the black Lincolns provided by the folks who had restored the homestead. He couldn't stand to sit next to Hildy Helen and feel her icy stare.

Unfortunately, he ended up beside LaDonna. Fortunately, after giving him one very full sniff, she concentrated on the scenery.

Rudy had to admit it was pretty here. He hadn't seen this much green and certainly not this many white dogwoods and shocking-pink rhododendrons since he'd moved to Chicago. Come to think of it, there had never been this many blossoms or this much green in Indiana. It was so lush, Rudy could almost feel it on his skin.

Although it was only a short way from Norfolk to Yorktown, Rudy had never been on a car trip this long. He was fascinated by the filling stations and hot dog stands and chicken dinner restaurants that popped up every few miles. He wished the driver would stop at one of the tourists' rests, but the Lincoln passed everything on the road and soon had them aboard the ferry for Yorktown.

"Even the cars are getting a ride!" he heard Hildy Helen shout as they all leaned over the boat rail to look at the bay.

"She's such a child," LaDonna muttered.

Says you! Rudy wanted to say. But he clamped his mouth shut and watched Yorktown grow closer.

If he'd thought there was a lot of "old family talk" at the train station, he hadn't heard anything like what went on from the time they drove off the ferry until they got to the old Hutchinson homestead.

There were relatives Rudy had never even heard of. Their connections to each other and to him were so confusing, he stopped trying to figure out which ones were cousins and which were aunts and which were several times removed, whatever that meant.

"Just call them all your kinfolk," Uncle Jefferson whispered to him. "Except the rich ones. You want to be sure you learn all about them. They might leave you money."

Rudy looked at him, startled. Uncle Jefferson laughed. "You're a true Hutchinson, all right," he said. "Enough integrity for an entire Congress."

Rudy didn't know what integrity was, but if it was a good thing, he was pretty certain he didn't have any. At least, Hildy Helen didn't seem to think so. Every time he tried to get within two feet of her, she would give Little Al a look and the two of them would move away. He could hardly concentrate on the tour of the mansion.

It was a mansion, all right, the Hutchinson homestead. It had been restored the way its new owners thought life had been lived in colonial Virginia in the eighteenth century.

"Now you know, of course," said the new owner, who was leading them around, her voice trilling up and down like an out-of-tune flute, "that the final, winning battle of the Revolutionary War was fought here in Yorktown. But before that, the colonists suffered. Oh, how they suffered. The British came to this very house and took all the Hutchinsons' supplies and food." She stopped at the base of a curved staircase with a shining banister. "The story goes that one of the British officers rode his horse right up these stairs."

"Fascinating," Aunt Gussie said.

It's history, Rudy thought. *Yuck.*

The lady led them through the back door and all through the house, pointing out the morning porch, the butler's pantry, the library, the sitting rooms, and the bedrooms. As the grownups oohed and aahed, Rudy looked over at Little Al, who was walking with his hands jammed into his knickers pockets, looking at the ceiling.

He doesn't go for all this history, either, Rudy thought.

Suddenly there was another thought—a voice, really. It was Miss Tibbs, saying, "If you had a different attitude toward history, Al would, too. He wants to be like you."

Rudy looked down and saw that his own hands were firmly planted in his pockets. He was pretty sure he had an expression identical to Little Al's—eyes at half-mast, lips hanging open in boredom.

I might not be able to get Hildy Helen over being mad at me, he thought, *but I think I know how to get Little Al back on my side.*

Cautiously he edged his way through the crowd of Hutchinsons as they followed Mrs. Flute-Voice—Mrs. McCrea, he thought her name was—out of the library and back into the entrance hall.

"This is where I found some things that I think you will all be particularly interested in," she trilled.

Rudy took a last step to put him right behind Little Al. "Wonder what it is," he whispered.

Little Al looked back at him in surprise, but didn't answer.

"These paintings!" Aunt Gussie said suddenly. "Are these—"

"These are your ancestors," Mrs. McCrea said. Her voice nearly went off the top of the scale, she was so excited. "The names are written on the back." She pointed to a painting of a stern-looking man with a square face. "Daniel Hutchinson. Son of Josiah Hutchinson, who came here to Virginia from Massachusetts with his family in the 1600s."

Rudy swallowed his dread of dates. "Wow," he whispered to Little Al.

Still no answer. But there was no dirty look, either.

"Now, here," Mrs. McCrea was saying as she pointed to a portrait of a group of people, "we go even further back. This tall, square-shouldered man is Joseph Hutchinson, father of Josiah, who was father of Daniel, whom you see in this other painting."

Rudy stuck his hand up. "What's he to us?" he said. Out of

the corner of his eye, he could see Little Al watching him closely.

"More greats than I can count, that's for sure!" Dad said with a smile.

Rudy pressed on. "And who are those people with him?"

"That would be his wife, Deborah," Mrs. McCrea replied. "Wasn't she lovely?"

Bridget giggled. "By their standards, I suppose she was. You wouldn't be caught dead with that hairstyle nowadays."

"The young woman is their daughter, Hope, who would be an aunt to you children. And the boy is Josiah. He was quite the man about Yorktown when he grew up, Josiah was. He built a huge shipyard, and there are several tributes to him in the local Episcopal Church—pews and memorials and such with his name on them."

"The Hutchinsons have always tried to serve the Lord," Aunt Gussie said.

Rudy's stomach, which had begun to relax, tightened again. It was that same thing he'd realized a few days ago—that he hadn't been thinking much about Jesus lately.

"You see there, Rudy, my boy!" Uncle Jefferson suddenly burst out. "See the eyes on young Josiah? They're a dead ringer for yours."

"They are, Rudy!"

Rudy grinned—not because his eyes were like some ancient Hutchinson's, but because the words had come from Hildy Helen.

"Maybe they are," he said.

"They are, surely they are!" Jubilee said. "Don't you think so, Jim?"

Whether his father agreed, Rudy wasn't sure. All he could hear was Uncle Jefferson murmuring in his ear. "There's your sentence, Rudy, my boy: a lifetime of honesty and fairness and wisdom. I wouldn't wish that on my worst enemy!"

His faded eyes were shining. Rudy knew he was joking. But

there was that tight feeling in Rudy's stomach again. *What kind of Hutchinson am I, anyway? What kind am I supposed to be?*

Suddenly he felt a poke in his side.

"Hey, Rudolpho," Little Al said, "what do you say we go out and explore the land some, huh?"

"I want to go!" Hildy Helen said. "Can we, Aunt Gussie?"

"You may," Aunt Gussie said, "if it's all right with Mrs. McCrea."

"By all means! This is your land in a way, too. This is Hutchinson land!"

Rudy couldn't help strutting a little as he and Little Al and Hildy Helen stepped into the bright sunlight behind the mansion. He was so busy looking over "his" land, he didn't notice at first that Kenneth and LaDonna had joined them.

"Oh," Rudy said, for lack of anything else to say.

"We're Hutchinsons, too," LaDonna said. "We want to see the land."

"Sure," Rudy said. He looked at Hildy Helen, who was nodding, though she was giving LaDonna a wide berth. You only hurt Hildy Helen's feelings once; she didn't give many second chances. Rudy was just glad he was getting his.

They made their way through a garden planted in neat rows with flowers Rudy had never seen before. The colors were so vibrant that he reminded himself to paint this picture when he got a chance.

"Now, I gotta ask," Little Al began, turning to LaDonna as they passed a row of ruby-red blossoms. "How come you got the same last name as Rudy and Hildy Helen when you're, y'know, Negro?"

LaDonna didn't even sniff this time. "Our grandfather, Henry James, was a slave down in South Carolina. His last name was Ravenal then, same as his owners."

"Owners?" Hildy Helen said. "How can somebody own another person?"

LaDonna's thinly tweezed eyebrows shot up. "Girl, don't you even know about slavery?"

"Oh, yeah," Hildy said.

Rudy glanced at Little Al to be sure he was listening, then spoke. "The Hutchinsons never owned any slaves. That's part of our history."

"And that's why, when the slaves were freed," LaDonna said, "my grandfather changed his name to Hutchinson. They were relatives of the Ravenals. The story goes that they helped him escape to Canada and then they found him again when it was safe to come back to the United States." She nudged Kenneth. "Isn't that right, Kenny?"

"Yes," Kenneth said in his frail little voice. "And he become a preacher, and Aunt Quintonia and our daddy was his chil'ren."

It was the most Rudy had heard the little boy say, and he found himself taking a deep breath for him. Then Kenneth folded up against LaDonna as if that sentence had worn him out completely and that was all he was going to speak for the rest of the day.

Little Al stopped and frowned down at a gardenia bush. "This garden is real nice and all, but is anybody else gettin' bored with it?"

"Don't they have any animals on this farm?" Hildy Helen said.

"It isn't a farm," LaDonna said primly. "It's a plantation. And I see some animals right over there."

She pointed, hand still in a white glove, toward a fenced-in area beyond the garden.

"Is that still our property?" Little Al said. "There's a fence around it."

"Of course there's a fence around it," LaDonna said. "How else would they keep the animals in?"

"Little Al never lived out in the country," Rudy said quickly. "He doesn't know about that stuff."

LaDonna sniffed, but to Rudy's surprise, she said, "I never lived in the city. Maybe we should just teach each other what we know."

She couldn't have stopped them all shorter if she'd dropped a wall in front of them. For a long moment, they all stared at her.

Rudy got his mouth to work first. "Sure—that'd be swell," he said. "Me and Hildy Helen know a little about both now, so we could help, right, Hildy?"

Hildy didn't look at him, but at least she nodded. LaDonna muttered, "Hildy Helen and *I*."

"Well, first off," Little Al said, "I always wanted to see a cow up close."

"There's some right there," LaDonna said. She kicked off her yellow pumps, removed her banana hat, and parked them on a garden bench. "What are we waiting for?"

Rudy couldn't stop smiling as Little Al hoisted the quietly whining Kenneth onto his back. They all took off for the fenced-in field. *Maybe it's going to be all right after all*, Rudy thought.

They got themselves over the fence, shrieking and tugging at each other, until all five of them were ankle-deep in clover. Little Al started to bolt for the nearest bovine, but LaDonna caught him by the arm.

"You can't just run up to a cow like that," she said. "You'll scare her to death."

"What do I do, sneak up on her? I can do that. I've had a lotta practice sneakin'."

"Watch me," LaDonna said.

Hildy Helen rolled her eyes at Rudy, who rolled his back. But he had to admit LaDonna knew her onions when it came to cows. She pulled up a handful of clover and, leaning over slightly at the waist, held it out to a nearby ebony cow. The animal stopped chewing and blinked her big, brown eyes at LaDonna.

"Pretty little dame, ain't she?" Little Al said.

"Who, LaDonna?" Hildy Helen said.

"No, the cow."

It didn't take a minute for LaDonna to have the cow eating out of her hand. Even Kenneth joined her and offered some clover. *He must feel more at home here,* Rudy thought.

He was feeling pretty much at home himself. He was, after all, a Hutchinson, and Hutchinsons had lived on this land a whole two centuries almost. He was starting to wonder if any kids had lived here, maybe a boy his age, when a shout shattered the air from across the field.

"Hey, you! Blackie!"

A red-faced man carrying a pitchfork appeared over the rise and stomped toward LaDonna.

"What are you doin'? Who tol' you you could come on my property?"

Hildy Helen looked frantically at Rudy.

"Say somethin', Rudolpho," Little Al said. "It's your property."

Rudy swallowed. "Uh, sir," he said. "She didn't know it was your land. We thought it was ours."

The man didn't stop, and even began to wave the pitchfork over his head. "I don't care," he cried. "She better get her hind parts off this land 'fore I take this pitchfork to her!"

He was now within a few feet of them, and his eyes lit on little Kenneth. Rudy watched as the little boy shrank into LaDonna's skirt.

"I don't want jigaboos around here!" the man shouted. "You know your place. Now get to it!"

The man's slurs seemed to hang in the air. Rudy's cheeks were on fire. He wanted to turn and run.

But this time, for some reason, he couldn't.

All at once everyone's eyes seemed to be on him. Not just LaDonna's and Hildy Helen's and Little Al's. There were those eyes from the old paintings of Hutchinson men with their intense stares. With their vows to serve the Lord, Aunt Gussie had said.

Rudy inched forward. "I think you should lay off, mister," he said. His voice faltered, so he took a deep breath. "We're Hutchinsons, all of us. If we trespassed, we're sorry."

He was sure his cheeks had gone from red to charred black now. Yet even as Rudy felt them smolder, the man with the pitchfork turned on his heel and without a word stomped off, back across the field.

When the man had disappeared over the rise, Little Al said, "That's tellin' 'im, Rudolpho." But he sounded as if he'd expected more.

"What was I supposed to say?" Rudy asked.

There was no time for an answer. Rudy felt his Hutchinson eyes widening at what he saw coming over the rise.

"What?" Hildy Helen said. And then she saw it, too.

"Run!" LaDonna shouted. "Bull! It's a bull! Run for your lives!"

Chapter Eight

*I*t seemed to come out of nowhere, that bull. From over the
rise the wide-shouldered animal dug its hooves into the
ground and came at them, head down and nostrils flaring. Even
over the screams of LaDonna, Hildy Helen, and Kenneth, Rudy
could hear it grunting and puffing.

There was no doubt about it. They were the sounds of anger,
and they had Rudy frozen to his spot.

"Run, Rudy!" Hildy Helen screamed from the fence behind
him.

But he couldn't—not until Little Al slung his arm around Rudy's neck and half dragged him to the fence. A pair of thin black
arms reached down and with surprising strength hauled him up
to the top rung.

"Hurry!" Hildy Helen cried. The desperation in her voice
jolted Rudy to life. He leaped down from the fence onto the
ground on the other side. When he looked up, he saw a pair of
big, flaring nostrils through the slats.

"Come on, 'fore he breaks down the fence!" LaDonna
screamed.

This time Rudy didn't hesitate. He even grabbed Hildy Helen
by the arm and pulled her with him. He could hear Little Al just

behind him with Kenneth whimpering on his back. Rudy kept his eyes on LaDonna, who ran before them like a chased deer, leading them all the way back to the morning porch.

They were all panting like bulls when they flung themselves onto the steps.

Voices rose from the porch.

"For crying out loud, what happened?"

"LaDonna, are you all right? Is Kenneth all right?"

Rudy looked up to see Dad and Cousin Jubilee clambering down the steps. Jubilee snatched up Kenneth, and Dad grabbed Hildy Helen and searched her face.

"We're all right, Dad," she said.

"No thanks to that fella with the pitchfork!" Little Al said. "He let a bull loose on us, Mr. Hutchie!"

"Why would he do that?" Dad said.

"Because he didn't want Negroes on his property," Hildy Helen said. "Rudy tried to tell him, but—"

Dad's eyes were on LaDonna. "You've had more than your share of insults these last few days, haven't you?"

LaDonna shrugged. "I'm used to it."

"No one should have to be used to that," Dad said. He shook his head. "That's part of the reason I wanted you children to come here to the homestead, so we'd have a chance to talk about what the Hutchinsons have always stood for."

Here it comes, Rudy thought. *Another history lesson.*

He cut his eyes toward Little Al. His brother looked back as if waiting for a cue.

Rudy sighed and sat up straight on the step. "So tell us, Dad," he said. "What have they stood for?"

"Help me out here, Jubilee," Dad said.

Jubilee pulled Kenneth onto her lap and smiled at them. "Your father and I are second cousins. My mother, Charlotte, and his father, Austin, were first cousins. And when they were about your age, they were the best of friends."

Dad's eyes got the yesterday look. "They used to tell us stories that would curl your hair."

Rudy thought, *Mine's already curly.* But he didn't say it this time.

"They had a lot of fun and got into a lot of trouble," Jubilee said. "But I think the most important thing is that, even as kids, they wouldn't let anyone be mistreated." She looked at LaDonna. "Especially not your grandfather, Henry James."

"I know," LaDonna said. "You've told me."

"It bears repeating," Dad said. "Charlotte and Austin taught Henry James to read, even though it was against the law."

"Reading *should* be against the law," Little Al muttered.

"More than once they kept him from being sold."

"They even helped him escape from his owner for good," Jubilee said. "Charlotte's own father—my grandfather."

"Now that took some guts, Miss Jubilation," Little Al said. "They musta been tough."

"Tough?" Dad said. He grinned at Jubilee. "Now, that is not a word I would use to describe my father. He was smart; he could talk about anything. And he stayed at a thing until he mastered it. But, no, he wasn't tough. He just had integrity."

There was that word again. Rudy didn't want to ask what it meant. He was pretty sure by now that he didn't have it anyway— no matter what Uncle Jefferson said. What did his uncle know, anyway? He'd met Rudy, what, an hour ago?

"So, you see," Dad said, "we Hutchinsons have always been committed to seeing that every human being is treated fairly. It hasn't always made us popular."

"But in the end, it's always made us happy," Jubilee said.

Rudy squirmed a little on the step and sighed. He was stuck in a history book again, being smothered by the pages.

"Enough of this for now," Dad said, standing up. "Why don't

you kids run off and see what else you can find, huh? Just stay on this side of any fences, all right?"

"And how, Mr. Hutchie!" Little Al said.

They all stood up to go, except Kenneth, who clung to Jubilee's sleeves and started to cry. Rudy felt relieved when Jubilee carted him into the house.

"Jumpy little fella, ain't he?" Little Al said.

"He's sickly," LaDonna said, driving her eyes into Al.

Al pulled his arms up over his head. "Hey, I didn't do it," he said. "I'm innocent."

LaDonna sniffed. "The river is down that way. I want to go down there."

Hildy Helen made a face behind LaDonna's back, but followed. They trooped again through the garden, then down a wide, sandy path with a ribbon of sparkly blue that beckoned at its end.

"What river's this?" Little Al wanted to know.

"Got me," Rudy said.

"The James River," LaDonna said.

"How come you know so much?" Little Al said.

"I read," LaDonna said pointedly. "You should try it."

Rudy watched the sting flicker through Little Al's eyes.

"It sure doesn't look like the Chicago River, does it?" Rudy said quickly. "Wonder if you can swim in it."

"Well, would you look at that," Hildy Helen said.

Rudy followed where she was pointing, then stopped dead on the path. To their right, in the middle of an endless green field, was an airplane.

It wasn't a three-engine Junkers by any means. It was a biplane, sporting two levels of wings connected by struts, with only one propeller. But it was a plane, and it was close enough for them to run to. Rudy did, without so much as a by-your-leave.

So did the rest of them, voices bubbling and chirping like

birds in a bath. Even LaDonna kicked off her yellow pumps so she could get there faster.

They all arrived out of breath. But Rudy talked anyway, facts spilling out of him like water from a bucket.

"This is a duster!" he said. "They use it on the crops. That's about a 400 horsepower engine. Look at that wing spread!"

"Fifty feet, tip to tip," a voice said.

They all looked up at the head that poked out over the top of the plane. A boyish-looking man pulled a pilot's cap off to reveal a shock of carrot-red hair and grinned at them. He had one of those mouths that seemed to contain more than the ordinary number of teeth.

"Are you the pilot?" Hildy Helen said.

"Of course he's the pilot," LaDonna said. "Why else would he be sitting in the plane?"

"Not so!" the man said. He shook out his hat and pulled off his goggles. His eyes were a brilliant, sizzling blue. "I can take two other passengers—non-pilots, if you will. Anybody want to go for a ride?"

Now this, Rudy thought, *really has to be a dream*. He turned to Hildy Helen, his heart pounding.

"Did he just ask if we wanted to go for a ride?" he said.

"Yes," Hildy Helen answered. She shook her head until the bob swished in front of her eyes. "But no thanks," she said. "I'm too scared."

"But *you're* not, are you?" The pilot was aiming his blue eyes at Rudy. "You've got a flier's heart, anybody can see that."

"I think I do," Rudy said. It still felt like a dream. He hardly recognized his own voice.

"You *think* you do?" the pilot said, leaning jauntily from the plane on one elbow. "Haven't you ever been up before?"

Rudy could only shake his head. He was afraid if he said too much, he would wake himself up.

"Well, let's change that! Hand over a dollar, and I'll take you up right now!"

"Just a dollar?" Rudy said.

"Whatta ya mean, *just* a dollar, Rudolpho?" Little Al said. "I ain't got a dollar! Do you?"

"No," Rudy said slowly, "but Dad does."

"Then go knock the old man over for a couple bucks!" the pilot said. "I'm finished dustin' for the day. I'll wait right here."

"You think he'd do it, Rudolpho?" Little Al said. "You think he'd give us two dollars so's we could fly in this plane?"

Rudy didn't answer, but his mind was spinning. Sure Dad would, wouldn't he? He knew how disappointed Rudy was when they didn't get to fly in the Junkers. And Rudy had made him proud in front of all those people when he'd asked so many questions about the Hutchinson ancestors. That thought stung a little. He hadn't been completely honest in doing that. But this was something he'd been counting on for a long time.

"Sure he will," Rudy said suddenly. "All we gotta do is ask him." He turned to the pilot. "Don't go away."

"I'll be right here," the pilot said. "I got nothing but time."

"Come on!" Rudy cried.

He took off across the field, Little Al right behind him. He remembered about halfway back to the house to look behind him for Hildy Helen and LaDonna. They were both walking stiffly, not talking to each other.

Rudy slowed down a little. "You sure you're too scared, Hildy Helen?" he called out.

She nodded firmly.

"How about you, LaDonna?" he said. "You want to go?"

"And where do you suppose I'm going to get the money?" LaDonna said, lip bunching up into a sneer.

"Can't you ask Jubilee?"

"No, I cannot," she said. Her head jerked up, almost sending the banana hat flying. Her neck suddenly looked two inches longer.

"All right, you don't have to bite my head off," Rudy murmured. Then he took off at a run again, straight for his father.

Dad and Jubilee were still sitting on the back steps when they arrived, joined by Mrs. McCrea. Rudy started rattling off the particulars before he even got to them.

And almost before he was finished, Dad was shaking his head.

"I'm sorry, Rudy," he said. "But that sounds far too dangerous to me."

Rudy stared. "Dangerous?" he said. "But you were going to let me—you were going to let us all—fly on the Junkers all the way from Chicago. We're just going to fly over the homestead."

"You're the one who's studied all the planes, son," Dad said. "You know there's a world of difference between that three-engine plane and some little crop duster. Besides, I don't know the pilot—"

"*I* do," said Mrs. McCrea. She, too, was shaking her head. The flute-voice twittered nervously. "He's fine at dusting crops, but some of the antics I've seen him pull while he's up there—flying upside-down and such things." She patted her chest with her handkerchief. "I wouldn't trust him with your children, Mr. Hutchinson."

"Then there you have it," Dad said. "Sorry, Rudy, but you'll get your plane ride one of these days."

"When?" Rudy said. "When I'm some old geezer like those people in the paintings—too old to have any fun at it?"

It was out before he could stop it. His face started going red even as the last syllable crossed his lips.

Mrs. McCrea busied herself refolding her handkerchief, and Jubilee excused herself to "go check on Kenneth." Dad, however, kept his eyes firmly on Rudy.

"That was uncalled for," he said.

"Sorry," Rudy mumbled.

"Are you?"

Rudy looked, startled, at his father. Dad's eyes looked awfully Hutchinson themselves—driving into him as if they saw things Rudy didn't want them to see.

"I'm not sure I know what to believe about you these days, Rudy," Dad said.

Later Rudy couldn't remember how the conversation ended, or even how he got through the rest of the evening. There was the huge supper in the dining room, table groaning with colonial dishes, the toasts to every Hutchinson who ever breathed, the imitations by Uncle Jefferson of various Hutchinson ancestors. Rudy sat numbly through it all, hearing over and over his father's words: *"I'm not sure I know what to believe about you these days, Rudy."*

When it was bedtime, Mrs. McCrea showed Rudy and Little Al to a room with big, heavy furniture. It had belonged to the John Hutchinson family when they'd lived there, she explained.

"His son Thomas was your great-grandfather," she explained. "Father to Wesley, grandfather to Austin."

Rudy tried to tune it out. But he couldn't ignore the fiery Hutchinson eyes staring at him from every wall, telling him he didn't have that Hutchinson thing after all. He excused himself and went to the top of the wide, curved staircase to sit.

I was just disappointed when I said that to Dad, that's all, he thought. *I can't help what I say when I'm disappointed.*

But that wasn't all of it, he knew. *Maybe I'm just a fake,* he thought. *Maybe I just pretend to be a Christian. Maybe that's why I haven't thought about Jesus much lately. Maybe all this time since I came to Chicago I've been trying to be like Dad and the rest of them—and I'm really just a joker like Uncle Jefferson.*

Rudy tilted against the banister and sighed. Uncle Jefferson wasn't such a bad fella, was he? He made everybody laugh. Aunt

Gussie seemed to love him, even if she'd never talked about him the way she talked about Austin, their grandfather.

"You're not giving up that easily, are you?"

Rudy flinched. The voice above him went into a soft laugh, and LaDonna sank onto the step beside him. She was wearing a green housecoat with feathers around the neck. Rudy had the sudden urge to sneeze.

"You're giving up?" she said again.

"What do you mean?"

"On the plane ride?"

"My dad said no. That's the end of it."

"Really? I wouldn't have thought you'd be that way."

"What way?" Rudy said. "I know he looks like he doesn't know what's going on half the time, but that's only because he's always thinking about his cases. When he says no to us, that's it."

"Oh, come off it," LaDonna said. She crossed her ankles and looked at him sideways. "I had you figured for the type who would never give up on something he wanted. I'm that way myself."

Rudy snorted. He couldn't help it. "You think I'm like you?" he said.

"All right, so I'm a 16-year-old girl and you're a 12-year-old boy. But we think alike."

"We do?"

"Think about it." She unfolded a thin, brown hand to reveal her long talons, currently painted red, and held up one. "First— we both hate all this talk about history and ancestors. The past is the past, am I right?'

Rudy nodded tentatively.

"Besides, they were ridiculous in the past. People owning slaves—it's disgusting. Why would we want to go back and pull all that out again and talk about it?"

She shuddered, making the feathers dance. "Ever since the war, all those old traditions and customs have been broken down.

They were just barriers to our happiness anyway. We don't have to be inhibited by them anymore."

"What's 'inhibited' mean?"

"You know, stifled. Like you wearing those old-fashioned high-top shoes. Don't you ever want to take them off and run barefoot?"

"Well, sure, but Aunt Gussie says—"

"And don't you sometimes wish that old bag of wind would just hush up and let you think for yourself?"

"Bag of wind?"

"Call her whatever you want. The point is, you want to break free from the past as much as I do."

"I do?"

"I've seen it on your face. I've been testing you, though you didn't know it. And you've passed with flying colors."

"I don't get it."

"You're a rebel, just like I am."

"I'm supposed to be a Hutchinson."

"And you are! They're trying to sell you a bill of goods about the Hutchinsons. Do you really think your ancestors have always been old sticks-in-the-mud like your father and Aunt Gussie? Bushwa! The Hutchinsons I know about—Austin, for instance— they were rebels. They did exactly what they pleased, when they pleased. They *lived*. And that's what you and I have to do if we're going to carry on the family tradition."

Rudy's head was spinning. "How?" he said.

LaDonna glanced around, then leaned toward him—so close he could see the tiny hairs under her eyebrows that she'd forgotten to tweeze. "I have some money," she said in a low voice. "Miss Jubilee pays me to work for her after school. That's how I buy my clothes. Otherwise Miss Jubilee would dress me like Aunt Gussie. Anyway, I brought some with me."

She searched his face for an answer, but Rudy was confused.

"So?" he said. "What are you going to do with it?"

"Not what am *I* going to do with it," she said. "It's what *we* are going to do with it."

"What are *we* gonna do?" Rudy asked.

She drew her lips into a smile. "Don't tell anybody," she said. "But tomorrow we are gonna go flying in that airplane."

Chapter Nine

*I*t didn't take more than a minute for Rudy to start nodding his head. Everything LaDonna had said made sense. And flying in that airplane was the first thing anybody had suggested in the last 24 hours that he really *wanted* to do.

"You know what?" he said. "I'm sick of being disappointed. And I'm sure tired of living in the past."

"That's what I thought," LaDonna said. She gathered up her green housecoat around her and blew a few feathers out of her face as she stood up. "Meet me right after breakfast at the field. I'll bring the money."

Rudy nodded again, then hesitated. "But—"

"What is it?" she said sharply.

"Well, I don't usually do stuff without Hildy Helen and Little Al. I know Hildy Helen won't go. She's too scared to fly. But Al—"

"I can't afford to finance the entire Hutchinson clan," LaDonna said. "Besides, he's so afraid Aunt Gussie is going to ship him off to prison, he isn't going to take any chances. I've sized him up. He isn't rebel material."

"Little Al isn't?"

"Nope. You're the leader of the group, like it or not. You're the one who has to take a stand."

With that she went off down the hall in a flurry of green feathers. Rudy was left with his stomach churning. LaDonna was the second one to tell him he was a leader to Little Al. Miss Tibbs had said it, too. If it was true, why did he feel like he was being torn in half?

It was a long night. Rudy spent most of it flopping from side to side in bed, plumping up his pillow with his fist and going to the window to see if the sun was coming up yet. Good thing Little Al was a sound sleeper—and a late one.

At dawn Rudy scrambled soundlessly into his clothes and took off for the field with his shoes and stockings still in hand. He had to admit it did feel good to run barefoot again. He looked behind him several times, but the homestead seemed to be fast asleep. He took the smoothness of his escape as a good sign.

The plane was right where they'd left it the day before, and the carrot-topped pilot was there, too, tinkering with the engine.

"Good morning!" Rudy called out to him.

The fellow looked up and beamed a smile. He seemed to do it automatically, as if Rudy had pushed a button.

"I'd about given up on you," he said.

Rudy shrugged. "It took us a while to come up with the money."

"The old man wouldn't come across with the dough, huh?"

Rudy shook his head. "But it's all right now. You got time?"

"If you've got the money, pal, I've got the time." Carrot Top stuck out his palm.

"I don't exactly have it with me," Rudy stammered.

"It's cash and carry, pal. No credit extended."

Rudy glanced toward the house. To his relief he saw La-Donna's silhouette approaching. "Here it comes!" he said.

"She's got the cash?" Carrot Top said.

"Yeah." Rudy's eyes narrowed. "You'll take her up, too, won't you?"

"Why wouldn't I? Long as she has the dough."

Rudy grinned. This part actually felt good. Finally LaDonna was getting to do something fun without anybody telling her she couldn't because of her color. It was an honest feeling, one that didn't turn his face red. As long as he didn't think about how he was going behind Dad's back . . .

LaDonna arrived, puffing air and carrying a pair of icy turquoise shoes that matched her cloche hat and the so-bright-it-hurt-your-eyes turquoise dress with its sash still untied around her hips. She already had two dollars folded neatly in her red-nailed hand, and she held it out to Carrot Top without a word. He looked at it, dazzled them both with his on-cue smile, and said, "All aboard, then. I got time for a quick run before I start work."

It was happening. It was actually happening. Rudy's heart was pounding so hard in his chest, he looked down to make sure his shirt wasn't throbbing in and out. He was really going to get a ride in an airplane, and the thought was so crazy, so fantastic, so out of his reach, he could only stand there and stare.

"You haven't changed your mind?" LaDonna said.

"Unh-uh!" Rudy said. That at least got his feet free from the spot and carried him to the plane. Carrot Top got down on one knee and locked his fingers together. Rudy blinked.

"Step into my hands," Carrot Top said. "I'll give you a boost up."

"If you think I'm going to get in that way, you got another think coming," LaDonna said.

"Then I guess you'll be waving to us from the ground," Carrot Top said as he hoisted Rudy into the plane.

Rudy looked down to see LaDonna sniff, stick her feet daintily into her too-turquoise pumps, and step into Carrot Top's hand. The pilot grinned the entire time, especially when LaDonna entered the plane headfirst, aqua sateen blowing out in every direction.

"He did that on purpose," she growled to Rudy as she righted herself.

Rudy didn't see that it mattered. They were going up into the sky in this bird. What else could be important?

Carrot Top seemed to take forever checking the underside of the plane and fiddling with this knob and that screw. Finally he hiked himself into the cockpit and pulled his cap and goggles on. With the flick of a few switches, the plane suddenly shook to life. Rudy's heart leaped right up his throat.

"Ready?" Carrot Top shouted over the racket of the propeller and the engine.

"Ready!" Rudy shouted back.

"How about you, Missy?"

LaDonna nodded.

"I'd hang onto that hat, then!" Carrot Top called out. "Because here we go!"

All of a sudden they were moving forward. Although Rudy's head barely cleared the fuselage, he could see things flipping by, even faster, it seemed, than they had on the train. There went the gardens, the mansion, the orchard.

It was several seconds before Rudy realized he wasn't seeing them from the ground anymore. He was in the air, heading up.

"Hot dog!" he shouted. "We're flying!"

"We sure 'nuff are!" LaDonna shouted back to him.

It was only later that Rudy remembered it was the first time he'd seen a real, true, honest smile on LaDonna's face. At the moment, all he could think about was the fact that they were airborne and getting more so all the time.

"How high are we going?" Rudy called to the pilot.

But there was too much noise, and Carrot Top didn't answer. That was all right. Right now the facts didn't really matter anyway. It was the feeling—that was what Rudy wanted to remember. He was so free, so above everything. It made him want to laugh, and he did, throwing his head back and hee-hawing into the wind.

He could hear LaDonna singing. It was magic. It was all perfect and magic.

They made a wide circle over the plantation, and Rudy craned his neck to see it through his glasses. The mansion looked like a dollhouse down there. It was amazing how straight the apple trees were in their lines. And, jeepers, that really was a big river. It made the Chicago look like a stream. He tried to capture it all in his mind so he could draw it and show it to—

Who? Who could he tell once they were on the ground again? He hadn't really thought about that, and he didn't want to now. He pushed the thought aside and let the wind whip at his face. He even took off his glasses and tucked them into his pocket so that nothing could stand in the way of that feeling.

"Are you hanging on?" Carrot Top shouted.

"Yes!" LaDonna said. "Why?"

"I thought I'd give you a few thrills. Hang on, now!"

Something Mrs. McCrea had said flipped through Rudy's mind, but there wasn't time to protest. All at once, the plane was climbing, climbing, climbing, almost straight up. And then there was quiet. There was no sound from the propeller and no sound from the engine.

"What happened?" Rudy cried. "Is the engine dead?"

"Are we going to crash?" LaDonna screamed. "Tell me we're not going to crash!"

Carrot Top didn't answer. He didn't do anything. He just sat, still as a post in the cockpit until Rudy was sure he had died at the wheel, and soon they were going to die, too. Frantically Rudy gripped the sides of his compartment and tried to lift himself up. Just as he did, the engine sputtered to life again. The airplane pulled up just above the ground, wobbling crazily.

Rudy's stomach lurched as he sagged into his seat.

Carrot Top tossed his head back and howled. "Had you going, didn't I?"

"He did that on purpose!" LaDonna cried. "Did you do that on purpose? Rudy, he did!"

But Rudy was too relieved to put up a fuss. LaDonna herself was laughing even as she scolded.

"How was that for a thrill?" Carrot Top yelled over his shoulder.

Still trying to stuff his heart back into his chest, Rudy managed a smile. "Aw, that wasn't so much!" he called back.

"No?" Carrot Top said. "Then you want to try something really exciting?"

"Sure!" Rudy said. He was certain there was nothing this airplane could do that he wouldn't love and wouldn't want to do 20 times.

"All right, then," Carrot Top said. "We'll try a little wing walking."

"Wing walking?" Rudy said. "You make the plane walk on its wings? Isn't that dangerous?"

"No, pal," the pilot said. "*You* walk on the plane's wings while I'm flying it. How 'bout it?"

"What's he saying?" LaDonna shouted. "I can't hear him. What's he talking about?"

"Wing walking," Rudy said, though he was surprised anything came out at all. His heart was back in his throat.

"What?"

"All right, pal, it's now or never," Carrot Top shouted. "I'm going to get us down low. You get ready. Get yourself halfway out of your seat, ready to crawl out when I say go. I'll hold her steady. You don't have to worry about a thing."

Rudy nodded numbly.

"Stay on your hands and knees until you get your bearings,

then stand up and walk! It's a thrill you'll never forget. I promise you that!"

"What is he telling you?" LaDonna cried.

But Rudy couldn't answer. His mouth was frozen. His face was frozen. His mind was frozen. He couldn't even *think* the word "no," much less say it.

The plane began to lose altitude, leaving part of Rudy's stomach somewhere up in the clouds.

"Are you getting ready?" Carrot Top called over his shoulder.

"Sure," Rudy said weakly.

Trembling, he got up on his knees in his seat and looked over the side. The ground was coming up to meet him, and his stomach—what was left of it—was spinning.

"When I say go, you go!" Carrot Top called.

"What are you doing, Rudy?" LaDonna shouted.

I don't know! Rudy's own head screamed at him. *I don't know what I'm doing! I'm going out on the wing of an airplane! I'm going to get a thrill! I'm going to get killed!*

Somehow, the moment Carrot Top shouted, "Go!" Rudy pulled himself from the compartment. The wind discovered him at once, snatching his cap off and yanking his curly hair straight up.

"Rudy!" LaDonna screamed.

But Rudy inched his hands onto the wing and felt his feet leave the compartment. Another moment, and he would be on the wing.

Swallowing, he moved forward. Suddenly he was out there with the wind whistling in his ears and the world whisking by below him—nothing between him and it but air.

For a second it was freedom. He wanted to stand up and hold his arms out and soar, just like the plane.

But when he got up on his hands and knees and looked up for a strut to hold onto, the plane took a sudden lurch. Both his hands flew out in front of him, and he slid wildly toward the front of the wing.

"Stop it!" he heard LaDonna shriek. "Stop it! You're going to kill him!"

But Rudy knew he was already dead. He dug his fingers in, but he kept sliding closer and closer to the front of the wing. Suddenly his head was past the edge of the wing, with nothing beneath it.

His fingers caught the edge of the wing and held on until the knuckles went white. He was staring straight down at the ground, at the dizzying rows of tobacco.

Jesus, help me! he cried silently. *I'm sorry, I'm sorry . . .*

He stayed there motionless, trying to breathe. His hands barely maintained their traction on the wing's smooth surface.

I can't move, he thought. *If I move, I'll die.*

Finally he started to cry.

"Stand up, why don't you?" Carrot Top called.

"I can't! I want to get down!"

"Get back in the plane, then!"

"I can't! I can't move!"

The pilot said something Rudy didn't hear, but LaDonna evidently did. She screamed, "You get this plane down *now!* That boy is scared clean out of his mind!"

"Hang on!" Carrot Top shouted. "I'm taking her down."

Rudy closed his eyes, squeezing out hot tears as he put his face to the wing and hung on until his hands ached. He could feel the plane heading at a slant for the ground, but it wasn't a thrill this time. He was sure he was going to throw up before they ever landed.

He was almost right. The minute the plane bounced and teetered to the field, Rudy held his head over the side and lost last night's supper. Colonial food didn't stand up to wing walking on a biplane.

When the plane finally jiggled to a stop, Rudy rolled off the wing, wiping his mouth on his sleeve and crying. He couldn't see where he was going as he stumbled away from the plane. That was why he didn't see his father until he had stumbled into his arms.

"Rudy! Rudy! Are you all right, son?"

Covered with mucus and throw-up and tears, Rudy nodded miserably, face pointed to the ground.

"Let me look at you. Good heavens, you're white as a sheet."

"I'm gonna throw up again, Dad," he said.

Dad pushed Rudy's head down, and Rudy lost yesterday's lunch, too.

"What were you thinking of, man?" Aunt Gussie shouted at the pilot. "You're an adult! These are children!"

"Whatever it was," declared Mrs. McCrea, "you won't think it again—not on my property!"

While Carrot Top was being fired, Quintonia and Bridget arrived. Grabbing Rudy from Dad, they began squeezing his arms and neck, checking for fractures. If he didn't have any broken bones already, he was sure he did by the time they were finished with him.

"LaDonna!" someone cried. That was Jubilee. She and Quintonia and Bridget together gave LaDonna a similar bone check, under shrieking protest from her. Behind them, another voice chuckled its way in.

"Now that was a good stunt, if I ever saw one!" Uncle Jefferson said. "You have some of that maverick Hutchinson blood in you, too, Rudy, I see!"

"Uncle Jefferson, if you don't mind," Dad said, his voice tight.

Rudy looked up in time to see Uncle Jefferson chortle into his sleeve and turn away.

Cautiously Rudy turned to his father. Dad's cheeks were pinched in, and his eyes had narrowed to slits behind his glasses.

Rudy tried to look down, but Dad caught him by the chin.

Rudy froze. The twins' father never laid a hand on them in anger. But the touch of his fingers now was harsh, and Rudy was afraid.

"Do you have any idea what kind of danger you put yourself in?" Dad said.

Desperate, Rudy groped for the right answer. "I didn't before we went up," he said. "But I do now."

It was the wrong answer. Dad took Rudy's face roughly in both of his hands and held it close to his own. "I knew before you went up, and I told you. Why didn't you listen to me, Rudy? Why did you deliberately disobey me?"

"I'm sorry, Dad, honest."

"That doesn't answer my question!"

Couldn't you ask it later, when all these people aren't standing here watching? Where's Hildy Helen? Why doesn't she bail me out?

It was a ridiculous thought, of course. With or without Hildy, Dad wasn't going to stop until he got an answer.

"I . . . I wanted to be a rebel—like the other Hutchinsons," Rudy managed to get out.

"What?" Dad said, anger contorting his face. "Where on earth did you get a preposterous idea like that?"

"LaDonna," Jubilee said sternly, "did you have anything to do with that line of thinking on Rudy's part?"

"Jubilee, that is absurd," Aunt Gussie said. "Rudolph is perfectly capable of making up his own mind. Don't put the blame on LaDonna."

For the first time since he'd landed, Rudy heard a familiar grunt. He looked up hopefully and saw Little Al standing beside Hildy Helen. He was glaring dead on at LaDonna.

But it didn't make Rudy feel better.

"It's not LaDonna's fault," Rudy said. "I made up my own

mind. But that pilot let her fly even though she was a Negro. I thought that was a good thing."

"Rudy!"

The word came out of Dad's mouth so sharply, Rudy thought he'd been stabbed with it. Dad's face was pale with rage.

"You're famous for weaseling your way out of scrapes," Dad said. "But how dare you use something we Hutchinsons have always fought for as a scapegoat for yourself! How dare you!"

"I'm not, Dad!" Rudy cried. "Honest, I'm not!"

"I cannot even discuss this with you now." Dad put his hands up as if to keep them from slapping Rudy. "We can talk about it on the train."

Rudy blinked. "What train?"

"We're leaving for home as soon as you can get your things together."

Dad turned on his heel, but Rudy couldn't move. If there had been anything left in his stomach, he knew he would have hurled it right then, right there, in front of everyone.

"We're leaving because of me?" he cried. "No, Dad—please don't do that."

Dad stopped, only long enough to glance over his shoulder. "We aren't leaving because of you, Rudy. We have far worse trouble than that waiting for us in Chicago, believe me. You've just made it a whole lot harder to deal with, that's all."

Then he shook his head and walked off toward the house.

✠ ❖ ✠

Chapter Ten

*R*udy stayed where he was until everyone else had gone except Little Al and Hildy Helen. LaDonna looked as if she wanted to come over to him, but with Jubilee on one side of her and Quintonia on the other, she could do little more than glance back over her shoulder as they whisked her off toward the mansion.

As soon as the grownups were out of earshot, Hildy Helen and Little Al made a beeline for Rudy. He waited for Hildy Helen to hug his neck and Little Al to punch him playfully on the arm—but he gave up that idea the moment he saw them at close range.

Al's face had turned hard and chilly. Hildy Helen's eyes were full of hurt.

"Wh-what's going on?" Rudy asked. "Why are we going back to Chicago?"

"What do you care?" Little Al said, barely moving his lips. "You're the only thing around here that matters, right?"

"I can't believe you were so selfish, Rudy!" Hildy Helen hissed. For a second she looked ready to cry. "Do you think you're the king of the universe or something? What did you think you were doing, going up in that plane?"

Rudy could only stare at her.

"Well?" she said.

Rudy cleared his throat. "You know how much I wanted to fly—"

"Flyin's one thing," Little Al said. "But pullin' some kinda crazy stunt like that? You shoulda seen Mr. Hutchie. He was close to blubberin' when he seen you out on that wing!"

"And what about us, Rudy?" Hildy Helen said. "Didn't you think we'd care? What if you'd fallen off?"

"But we used to pull stunts all the time!" Rudy said. "Little Al, you said you used to jump on the tops of trains on Clinton Street!"

"*Used* to," Hildy Helen said. She looked at him as if that answer should clear it all up.

"So what's that supposed to mean?" he said.

"We've learned not to do stupid things anymore," she said. "But it looks like you haven't."

"And what was all that hogwash about wanting to be a rebel like them relatives of yours in the paintin's?" Little Al said. "I bet none of them ever tried to walk on an airplane wing."

It was such a ridiculous statement, Rudy wanted to laugh. He wanted to shake them both until the real Hildy Helen and Little Al fell out. But somehow he knew that this time it wouldn't work. He'd pushed them too far.

He just stood there and stared at them until Hildy Helen tossed her bob and said, "Come on, Little Al. We have to finish packing." Little Al turned away, too, and marched back toward the house.

You'll be sorry! Rudy wanted to call after them. *I'll end up having all the fun and you two will be a couple of sticks-in-the-mud. I'm the Hutchinson who lives!*

But he didn't say any of it, because it sounded pretty stupid—even to him.

He dreaded going inside the mansion. But by the time he got

there, the attention had turned to the thing that was pulling them back to Chicago ahead of schedule. Rudy didn't find out what it was until he had thrown his clothes into his suitcase and brought it downstairs to set it with the others beside the front door. Uncle Jefferson picked it up to carry it outside, and he winked at Rudy.

"Don't worry, Rudy," he said. "They have bigger fish to fry right now. They've already forgotten your little escapade."

That didn't help, especially when Rudy heard Dad's voice in the library. It was nearly hoarse—the way it was when something was really wrong. Rudy listened at the door.

"I'm not afraid, James," Aunt Gussie was saying. "As long as Sol wasn't hurt, I've really lost nothing."

"Nothing?" Dad said. "Auntie, they blew up your entire garage! Your car was demolished!"

Rudy tried not to gasp.

"So, we'll build another garage and buy another car. I don't scare that easily."

"Maybe you should."

There was a pause, followed by a high-pitched answer from Aunt Gussie. "Is this James Hutchinson I hear talking?" she said. "The man who kowtows to no one when it comes to his principles?"

"It's one thing for me to risk getting hurt. It's quite another when someone threatens my family."

"Destroying my property while I'm absent is not threatening my family. Don't you know that if I thought for a minute that any of you was in danger, I would—"

She stopped. Rudy held his breath, sure they must be able to hear his heart pounding even through the door.

"Exactly," Dad said. "Now, in the first place, we don't even know who we're dealing with. It could be the owners of one of those companies where you're trying to get a union going. It could be some leftovers from the Red Scare, labeling you a communist."

"Go ahead and say it, James. We both know it's probably the mob. Al Capone has fingers in everything. He doesn't have enough to do selling illegal liquor."

"If there's money in it, he's involved," Dad said. "He's had it with me refusing to work for him. Then you come along and start fooling around with the unions he's trying to control. He probably figured it was about time he showed his hand."

"Well, I absolutely refuse to let this stop me from doing what I think is right," Aunt Gussie said. "Where is your faith, James? Doesn't the Lord tell us that as long as we are on His side, doing His work, we're protected?"

"It depends on what you mean by protection."

"James, I'm surprised at you. Since I've been here in this house, in the very place where so many of our ancestors stood up for what they knew was right, I've been reminded of our history. I have to take that with me. They trusted God, and so do I."

Dad sighed. "All right. I'll have my people start investigating this thing as soon as we get back."

"Just don't forget to pray, James," Aunt Gussie said. "The Hutchinsons have always prayed."

"Rudy, what are you doing now?"

Rudy jumped. Then he realized the speaker was Hildy Helen, standing beside him with her hands on her hips.

"I'm just finding out what I missed," Rudy said. He smiled sheepishly at her. "I'm glad you're speaking to me again."

"Don't count on it," she said. Clamping her mouth shut, she flounced off just as LaDonna entered the hallway.

"You're sure catching it from everybody over that airplane stunt, aren't you?" LaDonna said when Hildy Helen was gone.

"Yeah, I guess," Rudy said. He tried to swallow the lump that was forming in his throat. "Maybe I deserve it."

"Oh, don't be absurd," LaDonna said. She pulled her gloves from her turquoise satin handbag and thrust her fingers into them, red nails and all. "Look, we shouldn't have gone up in that plane this morning; I know that now. If you had been hurt, I never would have forgiven myself. I shouldn't have talked you into it."

"You didn't."

"Yes, I did. Would you have thought of it on your own? Who paid for it?"

Rudy gave an agonized shrug. "So I guess that means I'm not a leader after all. I'm more like Uncle Jefferson than I am like my grandfather."

"I don't know about that," LaDonna said. "But quit bangin' yourself over the head about it. It's over. We learn from it, and we go on."

"That's easy for you to say," Rudy said, his voice dragging the floor. "You don't have your sister and your best friend turning their backs on you."

LaDonna looked into the bull's-eye mirror on the wall and adjusted her hat over her Marcel waves. "While I'm here, I have no friends—period. Maybe you and I ought to stick together."

Rudy stared at her. "You want to hang around with *me?*"

"You're an interesting kid," she said. "And like we were all saying yesterday, we could probably learn something from each other."

Rudy didn't have a chance to answer, because the library door opened. Suddenly there was a flurry of good-byes, of people climbing into cars and waving out windows. He didn't know what he would have said anyway. It was nice of LaDonna to offer, but nobody could take Little Al and Hildy Helen's place.

There was no cheerful making-the-best-of-it on the train back to Chicago. Aunt Gussie, Bridget, and Dad huddled in their compartment and talked, heads bent seriously together, for hours. Quintonia, Jubilee, and LaDonna went straight to the sleeping car with Kenneth and came out only to ask for water, warm towels, and more blankets. Hildy Helen sat rigidly in her seat and read a Peggy Stewart book Rudy knew she'd already read three times. The worst part was Little Al, who took out his history book and pored over it, little beads of frustration on his upper lip, until it was too dark to read anymore.

I'm supposed to be helping him with that, Rudy thought as he watched from across the aisle. *Miss Tibbs was wrong. I'm not Little Al's leader. If I'm anything, I'm a sap. Now he'll probably flunk sixth grade, and that's my fault, too.*

Rudy thought the trip would never end. But when they got home to Prairie Avenue, he wished they'd never arrived at all. Where the garage had been at the back of Aunt Gussie's yard, there was only a charred, black hole, filled with the rubble that had once been the long, sleek Pierce Arrow.

"Dynamite," Dad said.

"I seen dynamite before," Little Al said. "Looks like a buncha long frankfurters tied together."

"Gussie, I am so very sorry," Cousin Jubilee said, patting her arm.

"Nonsense," Aunt Gussie said briskly. "That building needed to be leveled anyway. And I was tired of that black monstrosity we were riding around in. Sol!"

The old chauffeur looked up at her and blinked.

"See about getting us a new auto right away. Something in a nice color this time."

"Blue!" Hildy Helen said.

"Nah, red, Miss Gustavio," Little Al said. "I like a doll rides around in a red car."

Aunt Gussie peered at the sky, as if her new vehicle might be hiding among the clouds. "How about pink?" she asked.

"Pink?" Little Al cried, wrinkling his nose.

"After all, some people seem to think I'm a 'pinko.'"

"Gussie, you wouldn't—would you?" said Cousin Jubilee, clasping the front of her dress.

"I would, and I will," Aunt Gussie said. "See about it, Sol. In the meantime, I need to find someone to haul away all this trash so a new garage can be built for my new, pink automobile."

Aunt Gussie chuckled, a dry-as-a-leaf sound that didn't convince Rudy that she felt happy at all. He stuck up his hand.

"What is it, Rudolph?" she said. The mirth had already disappeared from her voice.

"I want to help," he said. "I can clear away trash, and we have three more days of our spring vacation left with nothing to do."

Aunt Gussie's eyes cut him off. "That's quite all right," she said. "I'm certain I can do this without your help, thank you."

Rudy felt as if he'd been stabbed.

"What about us, Aunt Gussie?" Hildy Helen said. "Can we help?"

"No, no—you children should be enjoying your vacation. I think a full agenda of movies and picnics and sightseeing is in order."

The kids all nodded, except Rudy. He only watched, bewildered, as Aunt Gussie turned her face toward him and added, "Besides, being amused seems to be what you do best. I certainly wouldn't want to interfere with that."

She left the yard then, walking stick thumping, hand tucked into Dad's arm. Hildy Helen and Little Al hurried after her, voting in loud chirps for which movies they wanted to see, which amusement parks they wanted to visit, which beaches they wanted to explore. As hard as he tried, Rudy couldn't swallow the lump in his throat.

Someone nudged him. He looked up miserably at LaDonna.

"Do you know how to ride the trains in this town?" she said.

"Yeah," Rudy said.

"Then get your hat. We've got things to do."

And things they did. There were 45 movie palaces in Chicago, and over the next three days, Rudy and LaDonna visited six of the most luxurious, including the Tivoli with its marble lobby, the Paradise with its statue of Eternal Woman, and the Uptown, that seated over four thousand people. They ate frankfurter sandwiches and drank vanilla phosphates after each show and talked about things like the antics of the Marx Brothers in *The Cocoanuts* and the bravery of Gary Cooper in *The Virginian*. Rudy told LaDonna she looked like a dark-skinned Mary Pickford, America's movie sweetheart. She told Rudy he was a dead ringer for Charlie Chaplin sometimes.

When they weren't seeing movies or talking about movies, Rudy was taking LaDonna to see all the important things in Chicago, things she shouldn't go home without gazing at first.

He showed her the houses in Pilsen, where the front yards were six feet lower than the streets because the streets had been paved over the debris from the big fire of 1871.

He took her to Navy Pier, where you could get a frozen Epicle treat any time of the day.

They visited the intersection of State and Madison, which the *Chicago Tribune* said was the busiest in the world. As luck would have it, they even got to witness a fender bender.

Rudy and LaDonna went to the steps of Holy Name Cathedral, where a famous gangster had been shot down. Rudy filled LaDonna in on everything that had happened to the Hutchinsons involving Al Capone's outfit since they'd moved to Chicago.

"You'll know them when you see them, Al Capone's men," Rudy said. "They always dress slick—black fedoras pulled down over their eyes. And under their jackets, they always have shoulder holsters with rods in them. A rod is a gun."

When he said that, it made him sad. Little Al had taught him all that gangster stuff. Now he wondered whether Al would ever speak to him again.

He was still feeling glum when they took a trip to the penny arcade below Van Buren Street, where there was an automatic piano and bulls-eye and pop-gun games. They shook their heads at the notion of getting tattoos—you could have them done in seven colors—but had their picture taken in a booth that said: "Postal Card Photo Taken in a Minute." When Rudy looked at the picture, he thought his smile looked fake.

Most times they rode the train, but once in a while they took a taxi. That was because cab drivers knew almost anything you could ask about the city of Chicago.

"You live in the Black Belt?" one of them said to LaDonna.

"No," she said. "I don't think so."

The driver snorted. "If you lived there, you'd know."

They had a couple of adventures, too. One day there was a downpour and they both crammed into a phone booth and watched the rain run down its glass walls in sheets.

But their most exciting adventure was one Rudy would just as soon have skipped.

It was Saturday. Rudy didn't have a plan, but LaDonna did, and she announced it to him as they headed south on Prairie Avenue.

Rudy was looking back wistfully at the receding forms of Little Al and Hildy Helen in the front yard when LaDonna said, "Today I want to see where my people live."

Rudy pulled his eyes away from his brother and sister and blinked at her. "I didn't know you had people in Chicago."

"Not kinfolk," she said. "At least, not blood kin. I'm talking about Negroes. I've been all over this city with you, and I have yet to see where my brothers and sisters live."

"Oh," Rudy said. "That would be the South Side."

"The Black Belt, like the cab driver said."

"I don't know if we really want to go there," Rudy said slowly.

"Why not?"

Rudy shrugged uncomfortably inside his sweater. "Because I haven't ever been there—"

"You're lying, Rudy. That isn't the reason. You're afraid to go there."

"Nuh-unh. I am not either. We can go."

"Good. Let's do it."

LaDonna doubled her pace. Rudy had to practically gallop to keep up. Being out of breath gave him an excuse not to talk so he could think.

I am scared to go down there! I'll be the only white person! What if they throw me out like that white policeman threw Quintonia off the beach?

He could feel his cheeks going red already.

By then they had turned onto South State Street, and almost at once Rudy's first thought came true. He was the only white person as far as he could see in front of him.

There were many open doorways along the sidewalk, most of them obviously saloons—though because of Prohibition, none of their signs said so. There were also some places that had once been shops, but had been turned into churches with Bible verses and crosses painted on their windows.

In every doorway, there was at least one dark-skinned person slouched against the door frame, looking as if he or she were guarding it against intruders. The curved bodies said, "I'm just relaxing here for a minute," but the eyes clearly warned, "but don't you try to come in without asking me first."

I won't! Rudy wanted to say to one particularly glassy-eyed old man. *You can count on that!*

"Let's go down another street," LaDonna said. "I'm not too partial to this one."

Rudy looked at her in surprise. The way she was clutching her little satin bag and holding her shoulders so straight, she didn't seem to be any more comfortable here than he was.

Rudy nodded and followed her west to another street, whose sign was missing. He stifled a gasp at what he saw. Before them was a long row of wooden houses that were minus more boards than they had. One had a large hole in its front porch. The one next door leaned into the first one as if it would fall down if not for that support—but there appeared to be people living in it anyway. They were the most dilapidated dwellings Rudy had ever seen, and there seemed to be no end to them or to the barefoot, bedraggled children who swung listlessly from their porch railings and watched Rudy and LaDonna go by.

This is where her "people" live, Rudy thought. His next thought—that perhaps LaDonna herself lived this way—stung him like a wasp from out of nowhere.

But it couldn't be. A glance into one house whose door was no longer there revealed a naked light bulb hanging from a wire in the middle of the front room. Another showed a kitchen tinier than one of Aunt Gussie's closets with one blackened gas burner on the counter. LaDonna clicked her tongue, but it wasn't disapproval Rudy saw in her eyes. It was sorrow.

"Maybe we ought to find us another street," she whispered. But they didn't leave before she dug into her handbag and pulled out a handful of change that she pressed into the hands of a pair of tiny, brown children hanging on a ramshackle gate. As they turned their little palms upward, Rudy saw that they were creamy colored, but the lines in them were entrenched with dirt like field rows waiting for seeds. He was glad LaDonna hurried to get away.

They crossed back onto State Street and ran smack into a tall, black man. He had just stepped from a doorway that reeked with greasy food smells and rang with music that scraped in Rudy's ears.

"Excuse me," LaDonna said to him.

Her voice was civil. She looked him straight in the eye. But it wasn't good enough for him. When she tried to get around him, he put his arm out and stared her down.

"Excuse me," she said again.

"What excuse you got, girlie?" the man said.

"No excuse," she said. "But I do have the right to pass. Please allow me to."

"Ooh—now this girlie got learnin' in her talk!"

"Yes, I am educated," LaDonna said, "which is more than I can say for you. Now why don't you run along and take some lessons in manners while my friend and I—"

For the first time, the man's deeply set eyes glittered over to Rudy. But even then, Rudy wasn't frightened. LaDonna was handling herself quite well with her "people," he thought.

It was a thought that lasted only a second. Two more men emerged from the smoking innards of the cafe and flanked the tall man on both sides. One wore an undershirt that was too tight. The other held a matchstick firmly between his teeth. Together, they couldn't have been any scarier if they had been a trio of wolves.

"Well, looka here," said Matchstick Man, without moving the match so much as a millimeter. "We got a white boy in the neighborhood."

"I ain't worried none 'bout that," said the tall one. "It's his high-soundin' friend here that's got my dander up."

The fact that they all turned their eyes back to LaDonna didn't stop Rudy's heart from hammering. He dug his fingernails into his palms as the men glared at her like nettled dogs.

"Now, I betcha she come down here to preach at us, don't you reckon?" said Mr. Tight Shirt.

"Well, she can just save her breath," Matchstick Man said. "We done had enough people talkin' at us 'bout hanging out on street corners and playin' in dance halls."

"How about talking like fools?" LaDonna said. "Has anyone spoken to you about that?"

Slick as grease, the tall man had LaDonna's arm in his hand, pulling her up to his face. Rudy froze, and Mr. Tight Shirt snatched him up by the front of his sweater and held him dangling above the sidewalk.

"Let him go!" LaDonna said fiercely.

"If I do, are you gonna get your highfalutin' self outta here, girl?" Tight Shirt said.

"Oh, but definitely," LaDonna murmured. "I've seen enough here, believe me."

Tall Man nodded to Tight Shirt, who opened his hand and let Rudy drop to the sidewalk. He picked himself up in mid-fall and dropped into step with LaDonna, who was already heading back down State Street in the direction they'd come from.

"Go on back to your white lady you work for," Matchstick Man called after them.

"And your Sunday school," Mr. Tight Shirt chimed in.

"But just you remember—you ain't no better 'n us, no how, no way."

They had left State Street behind before Rudy trusted himself to speak. He knew his face was fiery red. "How did they know you worked for a white lady?" he said.

"Because they could tell I wasn't some saloon maid or something like the women they associate with."

She walked even faster, and Rudy broke into a trot.

"It's too bad your people have to live like that," he said.

LaDonna stopped at the corner and scowled at the crossing traffic. "In the first place, men like that are not 'people.' They're a bunch of lowlifes who give the rest of us a bad name. When a white person runs into somebody like them, he just figures all the rest of us are like that, too."

The cars cleared, and LaDonna stomped across the street with Rudy in pursuit.

"Now, those children and some of the people living in those

rundown houses, they're doing the best they can, and most times they don't get the chance to better themselves." She shook her head angrily. "But those lowlifes, they don't even try to be respectable. I haven't got time for them."

"Right," Rudy said, for lack of anything else to say.

"But I'll tell you one thing for sure, Rudy Hutchinson." She stopped in the middle of the block and looked at him for all the world like Aunt Gussie did when she was about to lecture him.

"What?" Rudy said.

"I will never live like that. I am going to have a job and a nice place to live, and I am going to be treated like a respectable, middle-class citizen. You just hear me now."

"I do," Rudy said. "And I believe you. If anybody can do it, LaDonna, you can."

She tilted her head back so she could see him clearly under the brim of her turquoise hat. "I'm going to need to. I don't think I can count on even my family to stand up for me. I have to do it on my own."

Rudy's cheeks sizzled. *What was I supposed to do?* he thought.

"I don't expect support, mind you," LaDonna went on. "I know the way some people can make your blood run so cold you can't even move. I just have to be strong enough to—"

But Rudy didn't hear the rest. The minute they came into view of Aunt Gussie's house, everything was chased away by what he saw.

The front door was flung open, and three women with gray hats were being shoved onto the steps by a scarlet-faced Aunt Gussie.

✢ ⚜ ✢

Chapter Eleven

*A*s Rudy and LaDonna broke into a run, Rudy heard Miss Clara Blue Hair cry, "You are even worse off than I thought, Gustavia Nitz. You belong in an insane asylum!"

"First I was a pinko!" Aunt Gussie shouted back at her. "Now I'm a *crazy* pinko. You might be right, Clara, because here comes the proof!"

Aunt Gussie thrust her walking stick toward the driveway, where a car was pulling in with Sol behind the wheel.

It was a long, sleek Pierce Arrow. A pink Pierce Arrow.

As if Aunt Gussie had just proclaimed she was going to drive the thing down Michigan Avenue stark naked, all three gray-hatted ladies gasped at once and then flew to their own car—a boxy, gray Packard.

As their auto squealed off down Prairie Avenue, Aunt Gussie threw her head back and laughed. "Would you look at this!" she cried. "As I live and breathe, it's a pink car!"

"Gussie—you didn't!" Jubilee cried from the hallway.

She followed Aunt Gussie out of the house with Little Al and Hildy Helen jockeying to maneuver around them and get to the new vehicle. Rudy arrived just as they did. Hildy Helen made a point to step away from him. Little Al wouldn't look at him at all.

"Miss Gustavio, I don't know," Little Al said. "The Capone outfit is liable to shoot at you just for drivin' a car this color."

Aunt Gussie chuckled. "I knew I forgot something. Sol, we should have had them install one of those bullet-proof windshields like the gangsters have."

"Well, I'll say one thing, Gussie," Jubilee said. "I'm glad I won't be around to see what happens to you when you go into the city with this . . . thing."

Rudy gave a start. "Why won't you be around?" he asked.

"Well, because we're leaving for home tomorrow."

"Tomorrow?" Rudy said.

"That's what she said, Rudy," Hildy Helen noted with a smirk. She rolled her eyes at Little Al.

Rudy looked helplessly at Jubilee. "Can't you wait a few more days?"

"Well, no," Jubilee said. "I have to get Kenneth back to his doctor. LaDonna has to return to school—"

"But we haven't had time to do everything!"

"You're only going to have time to go back to school and take your exams anyway," Bridget said. Pulling at a reddish curl, she turned to Aunt Gussie. "Miss Gussie, since you've been thrown out of about every club you belonged to, does this mean I'm out of a job?"

"Of course not!" Aunt Gussie said. "Who do you think is going to help me fight these silly people with their ridiculous ideas?"

Bridget didn't look all that relieved. In fact, Rudy thought she looked about as lost as he felt.

Jubilee shook her head. "Like I said, I'm glad I'm not going to be around to see all this happen. I know you're a brave soul, Gussie, but I think you're headed for trouble this time."

Aunt Gussie didn't answer.

Quintonia put on a going-away banquet spread that night. It wasn't exactly a cheery affair. Kenneth sat on Bridget's lap and whined while she tried to get him to eat. Jubilee seemed so nervous she kept dropping her fork and knocking over the salt shaker. Little Al and Hildy Helen kept up their glares at Rudy across the table, and Dad and Aunt Gussie were both too preoccupied with their own affairs to look at anybody at all. They could have been eating fried shoe leather, for all they knew.

Rudy could barely eat. With Little Al and Hildy Helen rejecting him, it had been nice to have LaDonna's company for a few days. Now he wouldn't even have that.

On the other hand, maybe it was a good thing she was leaving. He hadn't stood up for her that afternoon down in the Black Belt. If she were staying longer, she would probably start giving him those same disappointed looks—the ones he was getting from people who'd thought he was a Hutchinson with promise but had decided he was nothing but a featherweight, like Uncle Jefferson.

"I'll be gone before you even get up in the morning," LaDonna told him before he went upstairs to bed. "Our train leaves before dawn."

"Oh," Rudy said. He looked down at his shoe tops.

"I'll miss you, too," she said. "Thank you for showing me the sights."

"Sure," Rudy said, still gazing at his shoes. "It was swell."

He wished later that he'd been looking up. Then he could have seen it coming and ducked. But he didn't, and LaDonna kissed him softly on the forehead.

"You'll figure it out someday, Rudy," she whispered. "Who knows? Maybe you'll turn out to be one of the best Hutchinsons that ever was."

She didn't stick around long enough to see his face go the color of a watermelon's insides.

It was long after dawn when Rudy woke up the next morning. Sunlight streamed through the window of the bedroom he usually shared with Little Al. But Al wasn't there, having taken to sleeping on the floor in Hildy Helen's room since they'd returned from Virginia.

Still, even before he could force his eyes open, Rudy knew there was someone in the room with him. When she said, "Wake up, sleepyhead, somebody's got to show me where the church is," Rudy sat up as if he'd been shot.

"LaDonna!" he said, staring at her. "Did you miss your train?"

She nodded.

"Aren't you going to get in trouble? What did you do, hide? Don't you think Cousin Jubilee will come after you when she finds out you're not on it?"

"Boy, you can sure run off at the mouth. If you'd hush up and listen, you'd find out that Miss Jubilee is on her way back home, and Kenneth and I are staying here."

"Here?"

"In this house."

"For how long?"

" 'Till we either grow up or Miss Gussie throws us out."

Rudy drove both fists into his eyes and then blinked at her. "You mean you're going to live here?"

"We are. Miss Gussie said Quintonia seems so much happier having her own kinfolk around her. And they have better doctors here for Kenneth and a better school for me, which Miss Gussie is going to enroll me in tomorrow. So she's having Bridget fix up some rooms on the third floor, and that's where we're going to live."

"But I thought you didn't like the third floor," Rudy said. His mind was still moving about as fast as porridge.

"I didn't like anything when I first came here," she said. "I was just showing my backside because I was mad at the world— after losing my mama and all that."

"Don't you still miss her?" Rudy said.

"Sure I do. But I wasn't as close to her as Kenneth was. They were just alike. Me, I'm different. I'm more like—well, I'm more like you."

"Me?"

"We both have someplace to go. We're going to make a lot of mistakes getting there, but they aren't going to catch us sitting on our tails waiting for something to happen. I am going to have a much different life than my mama had. And here in Chicago is where I'm going to find it." She smiled over his head. "I even prayed about it this morning."

"You pray?" Rudy said.

"Not much since Mama died, but I plan to get back in the habit. Don't you pray?"

Rudy looked at his knees, folded in front of him. "I used to."

"Well, you better start doing it again. You have to take me to church. Quintonia's going to stay here with Kenneth."

"Our church? Second Presbyterian?" Rudy said. He was suddenly picturing the three gray-haired ladies.

"No, I think we'll try *my* kind of church today," LaDonna said. "If our souls need to be revived, we got to hear some real, honest-to-goodness preachin' and singin'."

She wasn't kidding.

None of the dark-skinned attenders at the Walters AME Zion Church looked at Rudy as if he didn't belong there. They were too busy. From the time he and LaDonna walked in, neither Rudy nor the rest of the congregation ever sat down.

They had already started singing when Rudy and LaDonna arrived. It was more like shouting than singing, and the very rafters seemed to vibrate with the clapping and the swaying and the raising of hands toward the ceiling. Used to yawning through sermons at Second Presbyterian, where he understood only about every other word, Rudy was confused at first. But after about five minutes, during which he was shoved back and forth by the rocking congregation and coaxed into clapping by LaDonna, he couldn't help but join in.

When the singing stopped and the praying started, Rudy thought they might sit down, but no. Everyone remained on his or her feet, eyes closed, soaking in the prayers as if they were being poured on them from above. Their mouths weren't closed, though. Every time the preacher finished a sentence, the whole church erupted into "Amen!" and "Yes, Jesus!" and "Thank You, Lord!" Several times Rudy looked around, certain he was going to see Jesus walking among them, touching the hands they stretched out to Him. All he saw were faces streaming with sweat and tears. But he was sure that behind their closed eyelids they saw Jesus looking right at them.

The important thought didn't come to Rudy until after the sermon, which had some people down on their faces in the aisles, throwing themselves at the feet of the Lord.

If Jesus is here for these people, He must be here for me, too. I just need to go back and start over with Him. I can learn from the way I've messed things up—and I'll be happy again.

After all, the Hutchinsons had always prayed.

On the way home, while LaDonna hummed the last song they'd sung—and sung and sung until Rudy, for one, had a sore throat—Rudy whistled. He *was* happy, he decided. He was trying to follow Jesus again, and now LaDonna was staying, too.

They had a lot to do, he and LaDonna. He still hadn't taken her through the revolving doors at Dad's office building or to see the Italian marble that was falling off the sides of the Standard Oil building. And there was the Art Institute, his favorite place in the whole city . . .

Next morning, it was hard for Rudy to watch LaDonna go off to the high school with Aunt Gussie while he set out for Felthensal. But they'd get home about the same time, he reminded himself, and then they could get on a train and go exploring.

That was the only thing that got him through the day. It was the kind of day you needed something to help you get through.

For starters, Hildy Helen and Little Al wouldn't walk to school with him. They waited until Rudy was halfway down Prairie Avenue and then lagged along behind.

When Rudy passed Officer O'Dell, their policeman friend, the ruddy-faced man laughed and said in his Irish brogue, "So, lad, didn't you wash your teeth this mornin'? Is that why no one wants to walk with ya?"

Rudy didn't have an answer. He didn't feel like trying to explain his stupid stunt on the biplane, or the rift it had caused.

But he remembered when he had promised himself. *Jesus,* he prayed, *I know You're there. I'm gonna keep praying, because the Hutchinsons have always prayed.*

At school, Maury Washington picked up on Rudy's troubles like a vulture spotting fresh meat.

"Whatsa matter, Rudolph?" Maury jeered as Rudy passed the playground where the oversized bully and his three nose-picking friends, George, Clark, and Victor, hung around the empty bicycle rack. "Won't your brother and sister play with ya no more?"

Rudy didn't even feel like telling him to get lost. He tried to ignore the taunt and walked on.

Maury took another stab at it. "Too bad! Now you won't have anybody to play your nasty little tricks with, will ya? No, you won't, 'cause Alonzo and Hildegarde have taken your other friends, too."

Rudy couldn't help glancing back to where Maury was pointing. There were Little Al and Hildy Helen, surrounded by Earl and Fox and Agnes Anne. Maury was right—they were all his other friends. But from the way Hildy Helen was pointing toward Rudy and talking in whispers, he was sure they wouldn't be for long.

I know I did wrong, Rudy thought as he trudged on. *But do I really deserve all this? Jesus, do I?*

He decided to talk to LaDonna about it tonight. Maybe Dad would be another good person to talk to, or Aunt Gussie.

But the grownups were still so disappointed in him. It was as if all that was good in him had been erased from their minds, and all anybody could see was the bad. Anybody except LaDonna.

The minute he reached his classroom, Rudy was sure Miss Tibbs had already gotten the word about his shortcomings, too. There was a thick-necked man he didn't recognize coming out of the room when Rudy went in, but when Miss Tibbs saw Rudy, her eyes snapped.

You know I try! he wanted to say to her. *You know what I'm really like, don't you?*

"H'lo, Miss Tibbs," he said instead.

"Hello, Rudy," she said. It was as if she were only half there.

The worst was yet to come. After welcoming everyone back from vacation, Miss Tibbs plunged right into the history review. Rudy saw Little Al stiffen. He felt pretty stiff himself. Al's failure was going to be his, too—one more to add to the list Hildy Helen obviously was keeping.

"I believe we left off with George Washington," Miss Tibbs said. "Al, you were going to tell us what you learned over vacation about our first president."

Little Al plastered on a charmer smile that didn't reach his eyes. "He was our first president," he said.

"No fair!" Maury called from the back of the room. His nose-pickers nodded.

"I'm going to give Al points for being alert," Miss Tibbs said. "Now, what else did we learn about the Revolutionary War?"

Her eyes remained on Little Al, and Rudy could see him willing himself not to squirm or swallow or do anything that would show he was dying a thousand deaths right there at his desk. Watching the tiny beads of sweat on Little Al's upper lip, Rudy shot up his hand in a rescue attempt.

"Rudy," Miss Tibbs said, "if you are going to entertain us with some clever comment, please save it for your audience on the playground, would you?"

I don't have an audience on the playground anymore, he thought, shaking his head. "I wanted to answer the question," he said.

Miss Tibbs looked doubtful, then sighed. "Go ahead," she said.

"I learned that Yorktown is where the winning battle of the war was won. And before that, the British invaded people's houses and took their stuff—the Americans' stuff."

Miss Tibbs unfolded her arms, and her face got a little softer. "All right," she said. "Go on."

"I didn't learn this from the book," Rudy said. "I hope it's all right."

"Of course."

"My relatives lived in Yorktown, and one time the British invaded their plantation and one officer rode his horse up the steps—inside the house."

"No, he didn't," Maury called out. "You're making that up."

"Maury, hush," Miss Tibbs said. She smiled at Rudy. "Thank you, Rudy. That certainly makes history not quite so boring. That gives me an idea. Anyone else know anything about their family's participation in American history?"

Maury snickered loudly. "I bet Alonzo knows his relatives stunk up the whole West Side with their garlic!"

"Maurice, that is enough," Miss Tibbs said sharply. "Step into the hall, please. I have something I need to discuss with you."

Maury gathered his big self and rose from his desk, still snickering.

"Class, please write down all the family history you can think of while I'm talking to Maury. And no chatting, please."

When they were gone, and Rudy raised the lid of his desk to get a piece of paper, he felt someone looking at him. He glanced up to catch Hildy Helen watching him carefully. When their eyes met she looked away, but there was no angry glint in hers. Rudy's mood took a definite upturn.

"See?" he said. "I'm not just a clown."

Hildy Helen rolled her eyes. "If you were trying to impress me, Rudy, you can just forget it. I'm not like LaDonna, you know."

"What does that mean?" he said.

Miss Tibbs poked her head into the room.

"Rudy, no talking," she said.

When Rudy looked back at Hildy Helen, she was staring down at her paper, pencil poised. She didn't say anything else to him for the rest of the day.

Rudy was more than happy for school to be over that afternoon. He ran all the way home so he could get there before LaDonna did and change his clothes. Maybe they'd go see that Haymarket statue. She might understand it better than he did and could explain it to him.

But she had beaten him home, he saw that right away. She was sitting in front of the house in a blinding-white Stutz Bearcat speedster with its top down, laughing with a handsome boy whose skin was the color of coffee with milk.

"Hey, LaDonna!" Rudy shouted as he ran up to the car. "This is swell that you got to sit in a Stutz. This is aces!"

"I'm not just sitting in it, Rudy," she said, still laughing. "I got to ride in it." She turned to the young driver. "This is Clyde. He brought me home from school."

"H'lo," Rudy said.

Clyde shook his hand and said, "How do you do?" His voice was soft and low.

"I'm swell. Is he going with us?" he said to LaDonna.

"Going with us where?" she said.

"I don't know—wherever you want to go. We can't all fit in

this car, but we could take the train, like usual."

LaDonna shook her head. "I didn't know you and I had plans for this afternoon," she said. "Clyde asked me to go get a soda with him. I'm waiting for Aunt Gussie to get home so I can ask her."

"Oh," Rudy said. "Well—" He shrugged. "I like soda."

"You do?" said Clyde. "We don't want you to feel left out. Here." He dug into the pocket of his trousers and pulled out a quarter. "This ought to do it. You have a place around here you like?"

Rudy stared, confused, at the coin. Just then the pink Pierce Arrow arrived, and Clyde let out a guffaw. "You weren't kidding, were you?" he said to LaDonna.

"No, I told you she was the cat's meow, my Aunt Gussie," LaDonna said. "Come on, she'll want to meet you. And don't forget to be extra polite. She's very keen on manners."

They got out of the Bearcat and walked away. Rudy was left standing on the sidewalk with a quarter in his hand and no one to spend it with. He tossed it into the gutter and went into the house.

Even though he remembered to pray, that evening held a loneliness Rudy could hardly bear. LaDonna breezed in from her soda with Clyde, eyes shining. And after supper—during which she regaled them with all the details of how she and Clyde were among the handful of Negroes at the high school and how he had been at her side all day to protect her from the hostile stares of white students—she dashed straight upstairs to do her homework. Though she came down to the library to say good-night to Rudy, he felt as if she were only half talking to him. Her eyes were full of Clyde.

Bridget couldn't be torn away from Kenneth, who was in bed again with a fever and pains in his legs.

Sol had driven Aunt Gussie to another workers' rally, which

Quintonia insisted on going to with her, to "protect" her.

Hildy Helen and Little Al did their homework in silence, just a few feet from where Rudy tried to concentrate on his.

"What's this word, Hildy Helen?" Little Al said once.

She looked at it and frowned. "I don't know," she said.

"Let me see," Rudy said eagerly.

Little Al shrugged, not looking at him, and passed him the book with his finger stabbing the word.

"Constitution," Rudy said.

"Thanks," Little Al said.

That was the extent of their conversation.

By the time they were finished and Little Al and Hildy Helen went upstairs to brush their teeth, Rudy thought he would go crazy. He even lifted the cover from Picasso's cage, but the parrot only muttered irritably and covered his face with his wing.

"Come on, Picasso, talk to me," Rudy said. "Somebody's gotta talk to me."

"Feeling alone, are you, Rudy?"

Rudy jumped and let the cover fall back over the cage. Dad came into the library and put his briefcase on the table. He had already untied his necktie, and with a weary sigh he removed his jacket.

Rudy flopped into one of the leather chairs. Dad sat in another. Rudy looked down at his fingernails. Finally he spoke.

"Nobody'll talk to me. And I was wondering, was what I did so bad that everybody oughta treat me like I'm poison? I'm really trying to—"

The phone rang, jangling the rest of Rudy's words away. Dad put up one finger to Rudy and reached for the receiver.

"Hello?" he said. Suddenly he erupted from the chair, hand on the back of his neck. "You're where? Are you all right? Well, where are Sol and Quintonia? All right, I'll meet them out front.

Stay put! And Auntie, try to keep your mouth closed, huh? Just until I get there?"

He hung up and grabbed for his jacket.

"Dad?" Rudy said.

"Not now, Rudy. Your Aunt Gussie is at the police station. I have to go get her."

"But why—"

Dad stopped, one hand on the doorknob, and flung his other hand up impatiently. "Rudy, can you think about somebody else for one minute? Your aunt is in real trouble. Think about that, would you?"

When he was gone, Rudy dropped his face onto his arms on the table.

"I *was* thinking about her," he murmured to the table top. "I just wanted to know what happened. I guess I don't deserve to know that, either."

Chapter Twelve

*L*ate that night, Rudy waited at the top of the stairs for Dad and Aunt Gussie to come home. He figured it was the only way to find out what was going on.

When at last the front door opened, the first piece of information he gathered was that Dad didn't want Aunt Gussie going to any more rallies—ever.

"James Hutchinson, since when do I take orders from you?" Rudy heard Aunt Gussie say.

"I'm just trying to keep you from getting killed, Auntie, you know that."

"How on earth did I survive all those years before you came here to hover over me?"

"You didn't have the mob after you before I came here!"

"Tonight was just a little union upheaval—"

"My eye! It had the mark of Capone's outfit written all over it!"

"Those shots were fired into the air."

"And any one of them could have hit you, and would have if one of his men wanted it that way! This is racketeering we're talking about. I'm doing my homework, Auntie. Al Capone is working both ends. He's trying to get the workers in the unions to use

124

violence against their employers, and he's forcing the employers to pay him protection money to keep the workers from doing it!"

"I don't care about that. I only care about getting decent wages and working conditions for those women."

"Then do it some other way!"

"I will not!"

There was a long pause. Rudy got ready to take flight, just in case Dad marched up the stairs in a hurry. But his father finally said, "All right, then. Please don't go to any more union marches or rallies without me. Will you promise me that?"

"What are they sayin'?" someone whispered close to Rudy's ear.

Rudy nearly tumbled down the steps. It was Little Al.

"Uh—I'm not sure," Rudy whispered back.

"Why's Mr. Hutchie yellin' at Miss Gustavio?"

"Huh? Oh, she got in some trouble at the rally. I guess the police took her in so she wouldn't get hurt."

"They didn't rough her up or nothin', did they?"

"I don't think so." Rudy couldn't help staring at Little Al. Al gazed down the steps for a moment, then looked at Rudy.

"You think she needs us to help her?" he said.

"Us?" Rudy said.

Little Al opened his mouth, but quickly clamped it shut. Rudy felt his heart sinking.

"I guess I'll go back to bed," Al said.

"You can sleep in your own bed," Rudy said. "I'll sleep on the floor or something."

Al shrugged and slowly got up. He stopped on the top step and fiddled with the hem of his pajama top.

"Hey, Rudolpho," he said.

"Yeah?" Rudy said. His sunken heart took a leap.

"Aw, nothin'," Little Al said.

Then Rudy heard him pad off down the hall to Hildy Helen's room.

Rudy squeezed his eyes shut. *Jesus,* he prayed, *I really miss Little Al.*

It was the end of the week before Rudy got to talk to LaDonna again. Every afternoon she was busy with Clyde. Half the time she was running off to get sodas with him, which made Rudy think he'd be pretty sick of sodas by now if he were her. The other half of the time she spent sitting with Clyde in the library, listening to jazz on the radio and doing homework. Rudy knew *he* had never laughed that much while doing homework.

As Rudy's loneliness got deeper and deeper, Kenneth seemed to get sicker and sicker. Enthroned on the sofa in the parlor, he whimpered all day because his legs hurt and he had a fever. Dr. Kennedy came to examine him. The doctor chewed on his cigar a lot, like always, then shook his head and said he didn't know what to make of it. That was when Bridget went out and came home with a stack of magazines with strange-sounding words on the cover like "penicillin" and "hemoglobin."

"What are those?" Rudy asked her one day when he was at such loose ends he thought he'd drop off into space.

"Medical journals," she said. "Somebody has to know something about whatever Kenneth has. I'm going to find out."

Kenneth let out a little whine.

"You want me to go out and get him some ice cream?" Rudy said.

Bridget shook her red head sadly. "No, he needs more than ice cream." She ran her hand across the little boy's forehead and went back to her journal.

When Aunt Gussie wasn't supervising the building of the new garage, she was down at Dad's office, trying to figure out how they could prove what Al Capone was up to. That was all they talked about at the dinner table, too. Rudy thought if they didn't stop, he was going to explode.

In spite of his little chat with Rudy on the steps that night, Little Al didn't act any differently toward Rudy than he had since the day of the wing walking. Once in class he asked Rudy to read his paper about his family history, but Hildy Helen snatched it from him and said, "I told you I'd do it, Little Al. Rudy will just make jokes about it."

"I will not!" Rudy said.

"Get up and belt her one, ya sissy!" Maury hissed to him from the back of the room.

Rudy hunched his shoulders and pretended to read his history book.

"Maury," Miss Tibbs said, "remember what we talked about."

"Yeah, yeah," Maury said.

Rudy glanced back at Maury, just in time to see him give his three hyena cohorts a triumphant smirk. Rudy looked up at Miss Tibbs, but she did nothing. She just went back to the papers she was grading. Her eyes were troubled.

Why doesn't she haul him down to the principal for talking back to her? Rudy thought. *Why is she failing Little Al and letting Maury get away with everything?*

Then he remembered. The Hutchinsons had always tried to make sure everybody got a fair shake. And the Hutchinsons had always prayed about it.

Jesus, would you help Miss Tibbs be fair? I'm tired of things not being fair.

One thing Rudy knew for sure—with nobody else to talk to, he was remembering to talk to Jesus a lot more.

Recess was definitely no fun. It was bad enough that he had to hang around by himself, but Maury took to picking on him every chance he got.

"Hey, Rudolph," Maury said one morning, his pudgy face

beaming with evil delight, "why don't you go play jacks with the girls, since none of the fellas'll let you in on marbles?"

"Why don't you hush up and leave me alone?" Rudy mumbled.

Maury's thick lips smacked. "Because I don't have to. Miss Tibbs is in so much trouble with my old man, she doesn't dare punish me for anything." He looked at his trio of buddies. "I can do whatever I want, right, fellas?"

Clark, George, and Victor all nodded and narrowed their eyes at Rudy.

"Why's Miss Tibbs in trouble with your father?" Rudy said.

Maury's face mushed from smile to scowl in a split second. "None of yer beeswax. You wanna make somethin' of it?"

He pulled his too-big self off the top of the bike rack. George, Clark, and Victor cluttered around him, trying to look menacing.

"No," Rudy said. "Never mind."

But at afternoon recess that day, he stayed in and offered to help Miss Tibbs clean erasers.

She looked at him in surprise. "My erasers are pretty clean," she said. "But you can sure straighten the books on the shelves."

Rudy sat down on the floor and listlessly began lining up books' ends. Miss Tibbs wrote at her desk. The silence was deafening.

"You haven't been over for dinner in a while," Rudy said.

"Busy," Miss Tibbs said.

There was another silence.

"Could I ask you a question?" Rudy said.

"Mmm-hmmm."

"Are you really gonna flunk Little Al?"

"Pardon me?"

Her voice had taken on an edge that made Rudy look up at her.

"I said—"

"I heard what you said. Did you think that just because you

offered to help me I would let you pump me for information, too?"

"Huh?" Rudy said.

"I am really tired of being played like a piano!" she said. "Forget the books, Rudy. Go out and play—and tell Alonzo if he wants to know if he's failing, he should ask me himself!"

"But that's not what I meant!" Rudy said. "Why doesn't anybody believe me anymore? I pray, I try to help, I try to do what's right—and everybody still acts like I'm just . . . rotten! I'm sick of it! I'm really sick of it!"

He scrambled up from the floor, sending several volumes of ChildCraft tumbling off the shelf. They were still falling when he hurled himself out the classroom door.

"Rudy, wait!" Miss Tibbs said.

But he didn't. He ran down the hall, down the stairs, out the door, and onto the playground, where he threw himself down behind a tree and sat with his face in his hands.

That day after school, Rudy sat on the front steps at home and waited for LaDonna to arrive with Clyde. He didn't care what plans with Clyde were on *her* mind. He had to talk to her or he was going to go out of *his*.

When the Stutz Bearcat pulled up, Rudy prayed that she would just get out and run to the house. For once, his prayer was answered. She jumped from the little car without even opening the door and walked backwards up the driveway, waving to Clyde until the Bearcat was out of sight. When she turned and saw Rudy, her smile didn't fade. She was practically glowing like a light bulb when she plopped down beside him.

"Why the long face?" she said.

"Why the smile?" Rudy said. It didn't seem quite right to dump his story on her when she looked like this.

"You probably won't get excited about my news," she said, "but I have to tell somebody—and so far you understand me better than just about anybody else around here."

I'm glad you still think so, Rudy thought. *You could have fooled me, though.*

"Clyde invited me to go to the prom with him."

"What's a prom?" Rudy said.

"It's only the biggest social event of the year in high school. You get all dressed up, fancier than you ever have."

"That must be pretty fancy. You get dolled up all the time."

"This will be in a long dress, with gloves up to here." She patted her shoulders. "And he'll bring me flowers, and we'll dance half the night under the stars."

Rudy started to say, "Yuck!" but stopped himself. LaDonna's eyes were shining like a pair of moons.

"Is this part of that life you're gonna have that your mama didn't?" he said.

"You could say that, I guess, yeah."

"Then congratulations." Rudy stuck out his hand, and she shook it heartily. She also leaned over to kiss him on the forehead, but he dodged it this time.

"No kissing," he said. "I hate kissing!"

"You'll get over it," she said. "Are you gonna go with me to shop for a prom dress?"

"Do I have to?"

"No. I guess I'll ask Bridget."

"If you can get her away from Kenneth."

LaDonna shook her head. "I don't want to do that. He's been sickly his whole life, and I've been prayin' all this time that somebody would be able to help him. Maybe she's the one."

"She's not a nurse or anything."

"She ought to be. She studies enough. I think she likes that better than working for Miss Gussie." LaDonna looked down the street and gave Rudy a nudge with her elbow. "Now, I think I know what *you're* prayin' about."

Rudy followed her gaze to see Hildy Helen and Little Al meandering down Prairie Avenue.

"Yeah," Rudy said. "But so far—"

"So far I think it's working," LaDonna said. "Look how miserable they are without you. You hear me, boy—it's only a matter of time before they wake up. Meanwhile, you got me."

The door opened behind them, and Quintonia poked her head out. "Phone for you, LaDonna," she said. "It's that boy. Didn't he just drop you off?"

LaDonna smiled and sprang up from the steps. "He misses me already," she said.

No, I don't have you, Rudy thought when she was gone. *Clyde's got you. All's I got is—well, Jesus.*

When Hildy Helen and Little Al drew nearer, Rudy got up and went inside. He couldn't handle any more hurt today.

The next day was warm and summer-like. It made Rudy's heart ache too much to stay on the playground during lunch recess and watch everyone else laugh and run around with warm-weather abandon.

"I'm going home for lunch," he said to Miss Tibbs when everyone else had left the classroom.

"Will you wait a minute, Rudy?" she said. "I want to talk to you."

"I have to hurry if I'm going to get there in time to eat," Rudy said.

He left before she could stop him.

The pink Pierce Arrow wasn't in the driveway when he got home. "Aunt Gussie?" he called.

But only Bridget answered. Her voice was strange, strained.

"Rudy? Come here, would you?"

Rudy hurried into the parlor and skidded to a halt in the doorway. Bridget was sitting on the sofa, holding Kenneth and rocking him to and fro. The little boy was sobbing harder than Rudy had ever seen anybody cry, and he was shaking his head back and forth as if he hoped it would just fly from his shoulders.

"What's the matter with him?" Rudy whispered.

"It's the pain," Bridget said. "He'll hardly even breathe because his chest hurts so much." Her tightened face looked as if it were in some pain of its own. "He needs to be in a hospital."

"Hospital!" Rudy said.

"Yes, and now. Dr. Kennedy is off making a house call somewhere. I can't wait for Miss Gussie to get home. She's at a union meeting—Quintonia's with her and Sol. Your father's working."

"Aunt Gussie went to a union meeting without Dad?"

"I don't know!" Her voice was an explosion of frustration. "Would you help me, please, Rudy? I know you'd rather be doing something else. This isn't going to be a fun job, but—"

"I'll do it," Rudy said. "What do you want me to do?"

She closed her eyes for a second. "Thank God," she whispered. Then she opened her eyes and said, "Call a taxi."

Rudy did. Then, with his heart slamming against his chest, he helped Bridget put the still-sobbing little Kenneth in a blanket. Only his head stuck out, looking bigger than ever.

"It hurts!" Kenneth cried out.

Rudy was glad to run to the front steps and wait for the cab.

"Where to, lady?" said the cab driver as they slid inside his cigar-smoky taxi.

"Presbyterian Hospital," Bridget said in that strained voice. "We have a very sick little boy here."

The cab driver looked over the seat at Kenneth and shook his head. A long ash fell from his cigar. "They won't take him at Presbyterian," he said.

"They don't take children?" Bridget said.

"No, they don't take coloreds. Only place'll take him is Cook County Hospital."

"Take us there, then, please."

"Whatever you say, lady." The driver chewed hard on his cigar. "But I wouldn't take no kid of mine there, colored or not."

"What does that mean?" Rudy whispered to Bridget.

"I don't know," she said.

They both found out when they walked in the front door of the hospital on Harrison Street, not far from where Aunt Gussie had shown them the Haymarket statue. Rudy wished he were there now—or anyplace besides here.

The walls were a dingy green color, and the light from the naked bulbs on the ceilings did nothing to make them look cheerier. There were chairs lining the walls, but they were all full. There were people milling all around, some of them looking as sick as Kenneth. The air smelled like throw-up and rubbing alcohol, and Rudy had to hold his breath to keep from gagging. But he could do nothing to shut out the sounds—the men with crusty whiskers moaning, the scrawny, half-wrapped babies crying, the stiff-looking nurses barking at them all to please be quiet and wait their turn.

"We can't wait," Bridget said to one as she tried to hurry past them. "This little boy is dying."

The nurse scowled impatiently and peeked into the blanket at Kenneth. She came up with a different expression on her face.

"All right," she said. "Follow me."

They hurried after her, working their way around the pain-stiffened people with their empty eyes.

Is Kenneth going to look like that if we leave him here? Rudy thought.

The nurse took them to a room full of curtained-off cubicles and yanked one set of hangings aside to reveal a board-like bed.

"Put him there," she said. "I'll get a doctor."

Bridget didn't, but kept Kenneth cradled in her arms, kissing his forehead and telling him it was going to be all right. Rudy wasn't so sure about that. In the cubicle next to them, someone was shouting, "Somebody help me in here!" but no one was coming. There was only the sound of nurses barking and the smell of sickness.

"Rudy," Bridget said, "would you grab the journal I have under my arm and turn to page 25?"

For the first time, Rudy noticed that Bridget had a rolled-up magazine tucked into her armpit. He took it out and flipped to the page. "Sickle Cell Anemia," it said at the top. "Plague of the Negro Race by Dr. Herrick, Presbyterian Hospital, Chicago, Illinois."

"What's sickle-cell anemia?" Rudy said.

"It's what Kenneth has, I'm sure of it," Bridget said.

Rudy took a closer look at her. Her voice wasn't strained anymore. She was steady, confident Bridget again—and there was no sad look in her eyes like the one he'd been seeing for weeks. They were shiny green and sharp again, and she was once more lifting her head high as if she were about to take on the whole Al Capone outfit or something.

"Let me practice this on you, Rudy," she said, "if you don't mind. I want to be sure I can make myself clear to these doctors. What happens with sickle cell is that a lot of the red blood cells lack hemoglobin, which gives you oxygen. When oxygen doesn't get to your body tissues, your tissues hurt."

"That's why his legs hurt?"

"That's why everything hurts. His legs are about the biggest thing on him, so that's why he complains about them so much."

"Nothing's big about him," Rudy said.

"That's because when your parts don't get oxygen, they don't grow."

"Is he going to die?" Rudy whispered.

"If he gets a really bad infection from it, he will," Bridget whispered back. "It could affect his bones or his liver or his lungs."

"Oh," Rudy said.

He thought at once of LaDonna. She'd just lost her mama. Now what if her brother died, too?

"So was that explanation clear to you?" Bridget said.

"Yeah," Rudy said. "You said it really good."

"Let's just hope the doctors think so," she said. She put her face close to Kenneth's. His eyes were closed, and he was breathing as if he had sandpaper in his throat. "Don't you worry," she whispered to him. "I'm going to keep telling them until they believe me. I won't let you down."

Just then the curtain was whipped open and a very tall, very bald man blew in, white coat flying out behind him. Without a word to any of them he pulled the stethoscope from his neck and popped its ends into his ears.

"Don't you want to hear his symptoms?" Bridget said.

The doctor shook his head. "The nurse told me. He's suffering from malnutrition. Half of them are."

He tried to pull open Kenneth's blanket, but Bridget pulled the little boy away and tilted her chin up at the doctor.

"That is not Kenneth's illness," she said. "But why don't we start with some names? I am Bridget McBrien. This is Kenneth Hutchinson. And you are whom?"

The man said something that sounded like Dr. Mumble. Once again he tried to go after Kenneth with the stethoscope, and once again Bridget pulled him away.

"Do you know anything about sickle-cell anemia?" she said.

"Never heard of it," Dr. Mumble said, his expression just this side of a sneer.

"You're about to," Bridget said. "Rudy, show him the article."

Rudy stuck the magazine in front of him. The doctor gave it a hasty glance and glowered at Bridget. "What do you mean coming in here with some new-fangled junk and telling me how to diagnose patients?"

"Obviously somebody has to do it, seeing how you aren't keeping up. Sickle cell was discovered in 1910—right across the street at Presbyterian Hospital. Funny how you missed it, isn't it? It strikes about one in every eight hundred Negroes in this country. Since you seem to know so much about 'them,' you'd better listen up."

The doctor muttered something else under his breath that Rudy was glad he didn't hear. He snatched the magazine from Rudy and bored at it for a few minutes with his eyes. Kenneth whimpered in Bridget's arms.

"All right," Dr. Mumble said, tossing the journal onto a medicine cart. "Put him on the table. Nurse!"

She poked her head inside the curtain.

"You'll probably have to hold him down," he said to her.

"Over my dead body!" Bridget said. She put her face close to Kenneth's again and said, "I'm going to lay you down on this nice bed here, and the doctor is going to look at you. He won't hurt you. I promise I won't let him hurt you."

The doctor folded his arms over his chest and waited for Bridget to put Kenneth gently on the table. The nurse clucked like an indignant hen, and then her eyes fell on Rudy.

"What are you doing in here?" she said. "No children allowed unless they're patients! Out to the waiting room!"

Bridget dug into her pocket and pulled out some change. "Here, Rudy, get a cab and go on back home so you can tell the others where we are. Don't stay here in this place."

She didn't add, "It isn't safe." She didn't have to. As soon as he left the curtained cubicle, a pair of double doors in the hall flew open and Rudy was nearly mowed down by two white-coated men carrying a stretcher. The man on it was shouting, "Let me go back and get 'em! It's only a scratch! Let me go get the miserable dames!"

"Fell out a second-story window," one of the men said to a nurse.

"Mob at it again?"

"Search me. Looked like a bunch of women carrying signs to me. He was probably gettin' an eyeful."

Rudy was almost to the exit when the words registered in his head. *A bunch of women carrying signs.*

Miss Gussie's at a union meeting, Bridget had said.

Without Dad.

I'm just trying to keep you from getting killed, Dad had said to her.

"Where to, kid?" a cab driver said as Rudy climbed into his taxi.

"Do you know where there's a union march today?" Rudy said.

Chapter Thirteen

*I*t was true that taxi drivers knew everything that went on in Chicago. The bushy-browed man who picked up Rudy said it was funny he should ask.

"There's a meetin' goin' on now right over Randolph Street," he told Rudy. "I heard tell it's supposed to get rough."

"Can you take me there?" Rudy said.

"You like to be where the action is, eh, sonny?"

"Yeah, sure," Rudy said as Bushy Brows squealed the boxy cab away from the curb.

"Old Al, he don't like it when the dames try to get the best of him," Bushy Brows went on. "I heard tell his boys are gonna try and run 'em right off the street if they have to."

Rudy's heart quickened. "Run 'em off how?" he said.

"Same's they always done—guns, bombs, whatever it takes. Old Al don't care when it comes to his money, you know what I mean?"

Unfortunately Rudy did. He thought of the charred garage and the twisted Pierce Arrow. He pictured the wounded gangster on the stretcher shouting, "Let me go get the miserable dames!" He remembered Dad's words: "I'm just trying to keep you from getting killed." And he wished with all his pounding, aching heart

138

that he wasn't doing this alone. He wanted Hildy Helen and Little Al with him.

But then he remembered something else—again. *Pray. The Hutchinsons have always prayed.*

He hoped Aunt Gussie was praying right now. He sure was.

The driver could only get as far as Washington Street before a crowd of people standing in the intersection blocked his way.

"You'll have to get out here, sonny," he said. "And watch yourself."

Rudy dug into the pocket of his knickers for the change Bridget had given him, but the driver shook his head. "It was a short ride," he said. "Fare from that wouldn't buy me a frankfurter sandwich. Besides—" He wiggled his enormous eyebrows at Rudy over the front seat. "I done this same kinda thing when I was a kid like you. They had some riots in them days! Anybody ever tell you about the Haymarket riot?"

"Yeah!" Rudy said.

"I was there. Matter of fact—" He scanned Randolph Street a block away. "See that building on the corner where the fire escape is?"

"Uh-huh."

"That wasn't there back then, but there was a grocery store on that corner with an apartment over it. I climbed right up on the roof and watched the whole thing." He shook his head. "I always wished I'da seen who threw that bomb. I'da told, that's for sure."

Rudy bid the driver good-bye and slipped into the huge knot of people in the intersection. They were all buzzing and pointing to something ahead of them, but Rudy couldn't see a thing around their wide, tall adult bodies. The cab driver had been right—he was going to have to get up on a roof or something to get even a glimpse.

He looked doubtfully up at the tall buildings on each of the four corners. It must have been a whole lot simpler to be a kid back then. There was no way he could get onto one of those roofs.

But then his eyes lit on something that zigzagged like a line of Zs up the side of one of the buildings.

See that building where the fire escape is, the driver had said.

Of course, Rudy thought.

Ducking under elbows and shoving past shoulders, Rudy made his way to the nearest corner of Randolph and DesPlaines. He still couldn't see what was happening on the street. The crowd was even thicker here, and the jeering was louder, and there was no way he could push and shove his way through it. No one seemed to notice him as he grabbed onto the bottom of the fire escape and hoisted himself up. He'd climbed enough of them since he'd come to live in Chicago. Trying not to think of how many times he'd sat on one with Little Al, he concentrated on reaching the top.

What he saw when he got there made his heart pound even harder. The street itself was jammed with women, most of them dark-skinned. They were dressed in shabby sweaters, worn felt hats, and clunky shoes that would have made LaDonna click her tongue for sure. More than half of them were carrying signs that said things like, "Fair Pay for a Full Day!" and, "If We Can't Eat, We Can't Work!"

But that wasn't what nearly jolted Rudy from his iron steps.

It was the speaker on the platform across the street—a platform that looked as if it had been boarded together in a hurry and was only shakily holding the woman who stood on it.

The speaker was Aunt Gussie.

"No!" Rudy shouted. "You'll get yourself killed!"

Of course no one heard him except a startled pigeon who flapped frantically off the fire escape. Rudy wished he could do the same—and get down there and drag Aunt Gussie home before she was shot.

Rudy leaned out to look around. It didn't take long to spot a thug. A man in shirtsleeves and suspenders right across the street from Rudy's position leaned from an open window and looked down at the crowd. There was no shoulder holster on him, but Rudy knew from the way his head went back and forth as if he were scouring the crowd—and the way he kept his black fedora on, lowered over his eyes—that he was no sightseer.

Rudy looked around some more. There was another man in an almost identical outfit, no gun holster, leaning from another window farther down the block. And still another, also gunless, perched on a windowsill, stuffing pasta from a plate into his mouth as he watched the crowd. When the sea of women suddenly hushed, all three men leaned out even further. So did Rudy.

"All right, ladies!" Aunt Gussie's familiar voice shouted through a large cone that made it come out loud and echoey. "You saw the man fall out the window for looking at you—pushed by his own friends, no doubt!"

The crowd roared a laugh. Rudy didn't see what was so funny.

"That was intended to scare you, but you didn't run! You are not going to be controlled by anything—not by fear of standing up for yourselves, not by management that refuses to treat you fairly, not by the past that says you are inferior because you are women or because you are Negro. You are not even going to be controlled by the mob. You are going to stand for what is right—right?"

There was a cheer so loud, Rudy covered his ears. The three men in the windows didn't make a move.

What am I going to do if they try something? Rudy thought. *I don't know what I'm even doing here! Jesus—You gotta help me!*

The crowd of women quieted again as Aunt Gussie stood on the rickety platform with her arm up.

"I have asked you to gather here at Haymarket Square so we

can perhaps change history. You know the old adage—those who refuse to learn from history are doomed to repeat it. We are not doomed to repeat what happened here. We are destined to move ahead."

There was another cheer, which quickly quieted down.

"Ladies," Aunt Gussie continued, "I have been called a communist. But I'm going to do something now that no communist would do. I'm going to pray with you. Let us bow our heads."

A buzz went through the crowd, and for a minute Rudy was afraid they were going to turn on her. But Aunt Gussie waited, the megaphone in her hand, and Rudy could almost hear her thinking, *The Hutchinsons have always prayed.*

Slowly, almost one by one, the women bowed their heads beneath their hats. Some of them, Rudy noticed, even held hands. The watching crowd behind them shuffled itself quiet. Haymarket Square was as silent as its statue.

"Father," began Aunt Gussie. The word echoed from the megaphone so loudly there was no doubt that God heard it. Rudy was sure of that. "Father, we know that whenever two or three are gathered together in Your name, You are in the midst of them. We can feel Your presence here, and we pray that what we ask is what You wish to grant."

The words were like hands on Rudy—like Bridget's comforting hands on Kenneth. They rubbed away the lump in his throat and slowed his heart from thumping like a wild thing. Rudy suddenly felt so calm he rested his back against the hard metal of the fire escape and started to close his eyes.

But above the still and silent crowd, movement caught his glance. The man across the street was busy with something Rudy couldn't see, something below the windowsill. Suddenly he thrust out his arm and hurled that something from the window. It wiggled and waggled its way to the ground as if it had a will of its own, and then landed with only a spark.

Rudy whipped his eyes to the second man. He was launching a package of his own from the window.

So was the third man. Rudy squinted through his glasses. It looked like a bunch of long frankfurters tied together . . .

"Dynamite!"

The word had escaped his lips before he knew it was there.

"Dynamite, Aunt Gussie!" he screamed. "Run!"

But there was no time. Women began to shriek and shove and frantically paw at each other to get away. Several rushed onto the platform to grab Aunt Gussie, and before Rudy's horrified eyes the rickety structure collapsed into a pile of boards and bodies.

"Aunt Gussie!" Rudy screamed again.

But this time no one heard him. For there was a flash to his left, and one to his right, and one almost right in front of him. A *thoom* sound ripped through the air and filled it with pieces of hats and bits of shoes and particles of the street itself. And then there was nothing but screams and gray smoke.

Rudy covered his nose and mouth with one hand and tripped and stumbled his way down the fire escape, zigzagging back and forth with his heart nearly pounding out of his chest. But once he reached the bottom, he could see no better than he'd been able to above. The smoke and the chaos and the flames that licked at the buildings blocked out everything.

"Aunt Gussie!" Rudy screamed once more, though he knew it was useless.

Trying to push through the crowd was just as useless. People were shoving their way toward him like a mammoth, moving wall. When Rudy tried to get down on all fours and crawl between their legs, someone grabbed him by the back of his sweater and dragged him all the way back to Washington Street.

"Let me go!" he shouted. "I have to find my Aunt Gussie!"

"You'll get killed first!" the person said.

Rudy tore himself from his rescuer's grasp and turned around to stare.

It was Little Al.

"Come on! We gotta get outta here is what I say. We can't get to Miss Gustavio from here."

Little Al grabbed Rudy's sweater again. Together they elbowed and kneed their way down Washington Street to Clinton.

"We can't just leave her there!" Rudy shouted.

"We ain't. We can go around from behind."

He was still running, still dragging Rudy with him, and Rudy had to gasp to talk as he worked to keep up with Little Al's strong legs.

"How are we gonna get across Randolph Street?" Rudy said. "It's on fire! There's a million people—"

"We gotta catch a ride," Little Al said. He stopped at a wall—the same wall they'd looked over that spring day that now seemed so long ago, when Al had told him how he used to jump down on trains.

"If you know what I mean," Little Al said.

"I can't!" Rudy said.

"Sure you can. You rode on the wing of a flyin' airplane, didn't ya?"

"But I was scared to death! I threw up!"

"Who said you can't be scared? I bet Miss Gustavio's plenty scared!"

"I thought you gave up dangerous stuff like this," Rudy said weakly.

"This is an emergency," Little Al said.

From the direction of Union Station, Rudy heard a lonesome whistle.

"Just our luck," Little Al said. He fixed his eyes down the track, never taking his hand off Rudy's sweater. "Now remember I told ya, they're goin' slow when they come outta there. When I say we're goin', you just close yer eyes and come with me. I'll have a hold of ya. I promise I won't let go."

Rudy felt his breakfast surging toward his mouth. "I can't do it, Al!"

"We're goin'!"

And they were gone, off the wall and into the air, hurtling toward the top of the passing train—with Rudy screaming all the way.

The metal seemed to come up to meet them with a vengeance. Rudy felt the breath go out of him in a rush. He gasped to get it back and waited for the pain of hitting the ground, of being crushed by the train.

But Little Al was howling like a hound. "I ain't lost my touch, Rudolpho! I can still come through for ya!"

Rudy opened his eyes. The train swayed beneath him, and Little Al squatted at the edge of the dirt-brown boxcar, looking down the track.

"Come on, Rudolpho—you gotta pull one more stunt. When we get to Lake Street, we gotta jump off."

"Jump off? No!"

"Gettin' off's easier than gettin' on, but you gotta be ready. Come on, I'll hold onto ya."

Only the thought of being left on top of the train alone and ending up who knew where got Rudy to crawl to Little Al and squat on his toes. The train rocked as it picked up speed, and Rudy latched onto little Al's sleeve.

"I'm gonna fall!"

"That's the whole idea! Right about now!"

With one more mighty tug on Rudy's sweater, Little Al flew with him off the side of the train and onto the sloping ground beside the tracks. Rudy started climbing upward almost before he hit the ground—he was so afraid of rolling back under the wheels of the train. He scratched and clawed until he was on the side of the road.

But Little Al didn't let him catch his breath. "Get a wiggle on, Rudolpho!" he cried. "We gotta find Miss Gustavio!"

What they found when they rounded the corner of Lake and DesPlaines and looked down at Randolph Street stopped even Little Al in his tracks.

There was almost no one left on Randolph Street—at least not anyone standing—except the policemen who were looking down at the rubble beneath their feet.

They were gathered around a crumpled body covered with a cloth.

Chapter Fourteen

*L*ittle Al grabbed at the back of Rudy's sweater and pulled him. "Come on, Rudolpho. You don't gotta see this."

"But what if it's Aunt Gussie?" Rudy said. "Let me go, Al!"

Little Al didn't. He kept a firm hold on Rudy's arm until he'd pulled him, running, all the way down Lake Street to Dearborn. Then he steered him around the corner toward the Franklin Building, where Dad had his office. All the way they could hear sirens behind them, screaming in alarm.

"We have to find Aunt Gussie!" Rudy kept shouting over them. "We have to find her!"

Only when they'd reached the revolving door did Little Al stop and look Rudy square in the face. His black eyes were piercing, and his jaw was so clenched that he barely moved his lips when he spoke.

"You might be good at school history, Rudolpho," he said. "But you don't never look at the past we just been through. Ain't you learned nothin' from the trouble we been in?"

Rudy shook his head in confusion.

"I know better'n to try to handle somethin' this big on our own anymore," Little Al said.

For the first time, Rudy noticed that his brother's voice was shaking.

"That's why I lit out after you when you didn't come back to school after lunch and we got home and you wasn't there. I knew you hadn't learned nothin'."

"But how did you know where I was?"

"I didn't. But I heard Miss Gustavio was speakin' at that union meetin', and I thought maybe you'd try somethin' dumb—like tryin' to rescue her. After all, you're the guy who thought wing walkin' was a great idea."

Rudy felt his face turn red. "Why do you have to keep—"

"Never mind that now, Rudolpho. We gotta tell Mr. Hutchie. He's the only one can do anything about Miss Gustavio."

Rudy knew he was right. Feeling like a deflated balloon, he followed Little Al through the revolving door of the Franklin Building—and for once he didn't think about going around more than half a turn. The elevator arrow seemed to take forever to move to the bottom, and he thought they would never get to Dad's office on the third floor.

When they did, they saw a blurry figure behind the frosted-glass window of Dad's office door. But it wasn't Dad. The man who emerged was one Rudy had never seen before. He wore the uniform of a delivery boy, complete with brimmed beret. But he had a pencil-thin mustache, and his voice was deep when he said, "I was just making a delivery for Mr. Hutchinson. He's not in."

Rudy's heart sank. The lump in his throat was so big that he couldn't even cry.

"What are we gonna do now?" Rudy said.

"We're gonna learn from the past, just like Miss Gustavio said," Little Al told him. "It's sure easier doin' it this way than from that history book, though, is what I say." He pushed open Dad's office door and held out an arm for Rudy to go in. "We're gonna wait for Mr. Hutchie right here."

Rudy sank down into one of the wooden chairs opposite the desk where Bridget sat on the days when she was working for Dad. He stood back up again.

"I forgot to tell you!" he said. "We had to take Kenneth to the hospital. He has sick-as-something anemia."

"That sounds pretty awful."

"It is," Rudy said. "He could die. I'm supposed to tell everybody where he is."

"So call," Little Al said. "Maybe somebody'll know where Mr. Hutchie is—or where Miss Gustavio is. What do you want to bet she's home already?"

Neither of them believed that, Rudy knew. But he reached for the phone in the inner office on Dad's desk anyway.

After he'd asked the operator to put him through, Rudy stood with the phone receiver pressed to his ear and finally let himself think the frightening thoughts Little Al had been dragging him away from.

What if that was Aunt Gussie under that sheet?

Or what if she's in one of those ambulances we heard when we were running away?

What if we can't find Dad or Aunt Gussie—and Kenneth dies—and there's nobody to help Bridget?

But a voice suddenly came on the line. "Hello?"

"LaDonna?" Rudy said. His own voice broke, and in spite of the lump, he started to cry.

"Rudy?" she said. "What is wrong with you, boy? You sound like you got the stuffing kicked out of you. Where are you?"

"Is my dad home?" Rudy managed to say.

"At this time of day? Are you kidding? He's probably at his office."

"No, *I'm* at his office!"

"What on earth are you doing there? You better get yourself

home, boy. Hildy Helen said you played hooky from school this afternoon!"

Rudy didn't answer. LaDonna caught onto his silence like she was hooking a fish.

"What is it?" LaDonna said. "You answer me, Rudy!"

"Kenneth's at the hospital. Only Bridget's with him, and she promised she wouldn't leave him."

"Hospital?" LaDonna's voice went shrill. "What hospital?"

"Cook County, but—"

The phone clicked and went dead.

"LaDonna?" Rudy said into the mouthpiece. But there was no answer.

He set the phone back down on the desk and looked around Dad's office, his eyes blurred with tears.

I sure wish you'd walk through the door, Dad, he thought. *Jesus, I sure wish* You'd *walk through it!*

He sat in Dad's chair and swiveled it to look around, willing his father to emerge from a bookcase or a file cabinet.

But there were only Dad's books and folders. They looked a little disheveled at the moment. Usually Bridget kept things tidy when she came in, but she'd been spending all her time with Kenneth. Dad was always too involved in his cases to worry about neatness.

Too anxious to sit in the chair, Rudy got up and went to the bookcase. He started to push in a pamphlet that had been left sticking out between two books. Its title caught his eye.

The American Communist Party, it said on the front.

Rudy stared at it. What was Dad doing with a pamphlet about communism? And why was it stuck in there, instead of on the shelf with all the other pamphlets?

Stomach churning, Rudy left the pamphlet where it was. His gaze shifted to the top of the file cabinet, where something else seemed out of place. Another slim booklet poked from between some folders on top.

The Communist Labor Party, its cover jeered.

Rudy pulled back as if the booklet had stuck its tongue out at him. He glanced around the room, hoping not to see anything else amiss. But there, topping a pile of unopened mail on Dad's desk, was still another booklet.

This one Rudy picked up. *The Communist Manifesto in America* was its title. Swallowing hard, Rudy opened it. There was a bookplate glued inside the front cover: THIS BOOK BELONGS TO. Under those words, penned in violet ink, was the name Gustavia Nitz.

Rudy dropped the pamphlet onto the desk and tucked his hands behind his back as he stared down at it. That couldn't belong to Aunt Gussie. She'd said over and over that she wasn't a communist—she was only interested in the rights of workers.

Still, Rudy went back to the bookcase and opened the first pamphlet he'd found. Inside the front cover was glued another bookplate that said, THIS BOOK BELONGS TO: Gustavia Nitz.

The one on the file cabinet said the same thing.

"Hey, Rudolpho, you all right in there?" Little Al called from the outer office.

Heart leaping, Rudy stuffed the second pamphlet inside his sweater and dove for the first one.

"I'm all right," he said. "I'll be out in a minute."

He made a lunge for the desk and stashed the third booklet under his sweater with the other two.

"Did you get them?" Little Al said.

Rudy whirled to see him in the doorway.

"Get what?"

"Not what, who. Did you get Mr. Hutchie or Miss Gustavio or anybody on the phone?"

"Oh, no," Rudy said. He could feel his cheeks burning. "I just talked to LaDonna."

"Did she know where anybody was?"

"She didn't know anything. When I told her about Kenneth, she hung up."

Little Al dug his hands into his pockets. His usually confident face looked suddenly lost. "We got a lot of bad things going on, don't we, Rudolpho?"

Even more than you know, Rudy thought. But he was pretty certain Little Al hadn't seen him stuff the pamphlets under his sweater, and he was glad.

Maybe I can get rid of them before Little Al sees them—or anybody else.

But there were other, more chilling maybes that raced through his head. Maybe Dad knew Aunt Gussie was a communist and hid her literature here to protect her. Maybe dynamite had been thrown at her not because she was standing up for workers, but because she really was a "Red".

God, he prayed, *Please don't let Aunt Gussie be a communist.*

"Rudolpho," Little Al said, "we better get home. Mr. Hutchie ain't comin' here. It's almost dark."

"I don't want to go home," Rudy said. "Nobody's there anyway."

"What about Hildy Helen?"

Rudy shook his head. "Why would I want to go home to Hildy Helen?"

Little Al searched Rudy's face. "Why don't you love your sister no more, Rudolpho?" he said.

Rudy's mouth fell open. What was Al talking about? Before he could ask, a sudden jingling sound made him reach for the phone.

"Hello?" he said into it.

"James Hutchinson, please," said a crisp, female voice that sounded somehow familiar.

"Uh, he isn't here," Rudy said.

"I'm calling from Cook County Hospital. We have an employee of his here in the emergency room—a Quintonia Hutchinson?" There was some shuffling of paper. "How could that be? She's—no here it is, Quintonia Hutchinson. Same last name. Figure that one out. Anyway, she's here."

"Why?" Rudy said.

For the first time the voice grew suspicious. "To whom am I speaking?" she demanded.

And then Rudy knew. If she wasn't the same nurse who had chased him out of Kenneth's cubicle, then they all talked in the same accusing way over there.

"Why is Quintonia in the hospital?"

"Is this James Hutchinson?"

"I'm Rudy Hutchinson. James is my dad. We're all family. Tell me why she's there!"

"She got herself hurt in that union riot," the nurse said in an if-you-must-know voice. "You better bring your dad over here. Emergency room."

There was a click, and for the second time that day, somebody hung up on Rudy.

"I forgot all about Quintonia!" Rudy said. "She was with Aunt Gussie, I guess. And now she's hurt in the hospital!"

Little Al threw up his hands. "I don't care what nobody says about learnin' from the past. We got to go to her, Rudolpho, seein' how we don't know where anybody else is! I know a shortcut—"

But Rudy dug into his pocket and pulled out the change Bridget had given him. "A cab'll be quicker," he said.

It was almost completely dark when they pulled up in front of Cook County Hospital. That only made the place dingier and more frightening. The moment they walked through the front door, Little Al put his hand over his nose. "I hate hospitals," he said. "They stink!"

Rudy just held his breath until they reached the desk, behind which sat the stiff nurse. Her eyes hardened when she saw Rudy.

"We came to see Quintonia Hutchinson," he said.

"You and who else?" she said, eyes glittering suspiciously at Little Al.

"Just me and him."

"You can't go in without an adult," she said. "I already told you once today, no children are allowed back there." She made her disapproving hen-clucking sound. "How many coloreds do you know, anyhow? You look like a well-off boy. Seems like you'd find somebody better to associate with."

"There isn't anybody better!" Rudy shouted at her.

She shrank back for a second, long enough for Rudy to bite at his lip and hope he hadn't really said it out loud. But behind him, Little Al leaned in close to his ear and whispered, "Atta boy, Rudolpho. You tell her!"

The nurse recovered quickly and half rose from the chair. "Keep your voice down and mind your manners!" she said. "Or I will have you thrown out of here altogether. Now go and sit on those chairs over there until a grownup joins you, and then I will give that person the information you want."

"There's no need to wait," said a voice behind them. "I'm the grownup."

Rudy turned around. LaDonna put her long fingers on his shoulder. "Now, where is Kenneth Hutchinson?" she said to the nurse.

✣ ✣ ✣

Chapter Fifteen

*T*he nurse's eyebrows rose, but she kept the suspicious gleam in her eyes.

"Kenneth Hutchinson?" she said. "These boys were looking for *Quintonia* Hutchinson."

LaDonna's hand gripped Rudy's shoulder. "Aunt Quintonia? What's wrong? Is she sick, too?"

"She was with Aunt Gussie. There was a union rally—and there was dynamite. I saw it! I tried to warn her, but there was nothing left but a body when we got back there. And I'm afraid Aunt Gussie's dead—or else she really is a communist or something!"

LaDonna put a gentle hand over Rudy's mouth. Then, taking the hand away, she bent down and pulled him to her shoulder. It felt safe to cry there, and he did.

"Hush, now," she whispered. "You just be brave. We Hutchinsons are always brave . . . I think."

The nurse tapped her pencil on the desktop. "So now you expect me to believe that you are related?"

"I don't need questions from you," LaDonna said above Rudy's head. "I just need answers. Where is my brother, Kenneth Hutchinson? And where is my aunt, Quintonia Hutchinson?"

And where is my *aunt, Gustavia Nitz?* Rudy thought. But he knew Aunt Gussie wouldn't be here. They would have taken her to—what was that other hospital? Presbyterian?

"Your brother has been moved upstairs to the pediatric ward," the nurse was saying between gritted teeth. "And your aunt is in cubicle number four. But this *child* cannot go back there with you."

Rudy pushed back from LaDonna and stood on tiptoes to get close to her ear. "That's all right," he said. "Me and Little Al will go over to Presbyterian Hospital and try to find Aunt Gussie."

"You and Little Al?" LaDonna said. "Where is he?"

Rudy whipped his head around. Little Al was nowhere to be seen.

"Clyde, I'm going to go on back and see my brother," LaDonna said. "Thank you for bringing me. You can go on now."

Rudy realized for the first time that handsome Clyde was standing nearby, hat in his hands.

"I won't leave," Clyde said in his soft, low voice. "You go on. I'll just wait out here."

LaDonna nodded and gave Rudy's shoulder a final squeeze before she hurried off to cubicle number four. Rudy's mind was reeling. As soon as she was out of sight, Rudy turned to Clyde. "You want to be my other grownup?" he said.

"What do you mean?"

"Could you find out where Kenneth is and go up and see him and come back and tell me if—if he's—"

"I'll come back and tell you he's just fine," Clyde said. He ambled over to the desk and leaned politely over the nurse.

No wonder LaDonna likes him so much, Rudy thought. He smeared the last of the tears off his cheeks. Maybe it was going to be all right after all. But if it was, he would have to help make it that way.

After a reassuring wink in Rudy's direction, Clyde headed up

the stairs. Rudy turned toward the front door. Little Al was probably way ahead of him, halfway to Presbyterian Hospital by now.

But a familiar "Psst!" stopped him and made him look around.

That sure sounded like Little Al. But Rudy didn't see him anywhere. He was about to take off again when the "Psst" came
louder, and was followed by a whispered, nasal "Rudolpho!"

It seemed to come from the direction of a large cart piled with
soiled sheets. Something else was coming from it, too—a powerful stink that made Rudy want to plug his nose.

"In here!" the cart hissed.

Looking over both shoulders and seeing that the nurse was
busy interrogating some other poor soul, Rudy went for the cart.
A hand reached out from under the foul sheets and grabbed him.

"Get in!" he heard Little Al whisper. "And hurry up before
somebody sees you!"

Giving the waiting room one more hurried glance, Rudy decided all the people there were too sick or tired or discouraged
to even lift their eyes. He climbed under the sheets, where Little
Al had his fingers clamped firmly over his nose. Rudy did the
same.

"I tol' you I hate hosbidals," Little Al muttered.

"What are we doing?" Rudy whispered.

"We're gonna find Kenneth and Quintonia."

"They've already been found! LaDonna and Clyde are with
them."

"Oh," Little Al said. "Well, that's good. That means we don't
have to ride around in this disgusting thing."

But just then, the disgusting thing lurched, and they were
suddenly rolling down the hall.

"Uh-oh," Little Al whispered.

"Yeah," Rudy whispered back.

Whoever was pushing the cart was in a hurry, because the
thing careened around every corner on two wheels and took the

straightaways faster than Sol usually drove the Pierce Arrow.

"He drives like a cabbie," Little Al whispered.

There was a sudden stop—then a loud grunt, which told Rudy their driver was a man. All at once the cart tilted on one end and began to bounce noisily.

"Ow! He's hauling us upstairs, for Pete's sake!" Little Al whispered.

"That's where Kenneth and Bridget are! Let's jump out first chance we get."

"That's what I say, too."

The cart finally stopped, and the driver grunted as he walked away. Little Al rose slightly and peeked out from between two rumpled pillow cases.

"All clear!" he hissed.

With a heave of dirty linen, they scrambled from the cart, not bothering to stuff any of it back in for fear Grunting Man would discover them and throw them both down the laundry chute with the rest of it.

Little Al took off down the hall. Rudy followed, looking up at the dreary green walls and seeing that there were words and arrows printed on them.

MATERNITY, one said, whatever that meant.

SURGERY, said another.

"What do you call a kids' ward, Rudolpho?" Little Al asked.

"I think that nurse said—"

Just then there was an angry voice behind them. "Hey, who did this?"

They both whirled around to see a large cube of a man standing at the cart, glaring, red-faced, at the trail of sheets Rudy and Little Al had left behind. He looked up and locked eyes with Rudy.

"Was it you? Hey, what are you kids doin' up here? You ain't supposed to be up here!"

"Run, Rudolpho!" Little Al cried.

Rudy didn't have to be told twice. He bolted around the corner, where the arrow said SURGERY. He looked around frantically for an open door. There was one just a few feet down. Heart in his throat, he made a run for it and hurled himself inside. He ran straight into a tray-carrying nurse, sending bottles of pills flying everywhere. Rudy nearly slipped on them as he made an about-face and retreated.

The nurse was not so fortunate. Rudy heard her squeal before he heard the thud as she hit the floor.

He reached down and snatched a bottle of pink tablets which had rolled his way. Unscrewing the lid, he dumped the pills onto the hall floor and took off.

"Stop, ya little brat!" he heard Grunting Man yell behind him.

Rudy glanced over his shoulder in time to see him slide crazily on the pills and topple to the floor.

"Sorry!" Rudy called out. He dove around another corner and nearly collided with a stretcher on wheels. There was someone on it who looked to be more bandages than person. Rudy dodged it and searched for another open doorway.

"Somebody get that kid!" Grunting Man cried from around the corner.

"What kid?" said a woman's voice—a nurse, Rudy guessed.

Rudy dove under the stretcher cart and pulled the overhanging sheet in front of him—just before he heard the big, cube-like man grunt his way around the corner.

"Where is he?" the man said.

"Where's who?" said the woman's voice. "Maybe we ought to find a bed for *you*, Clarence. You're starting to see things."

"I did not see things. There were two kids running around up here. They stole up in my linen cart."

"Oh, so now there are two of them." The woman laughed. "Go have a cup of coffee, Clarence. Not only are you seeing things, you're seeing things double!"

She laughed again. Grunting Man grunted.

After a minute Rudy couldn't hear either of them anymore. He peeked out from behind the sheet. The hallway was empty.

Where's Little Al? Rudy thought. This wasn't getting them any closer to Aunt Gussie, and she was the one he was worried about—in more ways than one.

After making sure that the hall was still empty, he stuck his head further out from under the sheet.

"Al?" he whispered. "Are you there?"

"I don't think he is," said a weak voice. "But I most certainly am. Now get out from under there and call Dr. Kennedy."

Rudy couldn't get out fast enough.

"Aunt Gussie?" he said.

Even looking at the figure on the stretcher, it was hard to tell. The face was completely swathed in bandages, except for the eyes. Rudy knew those belonged to his aunt. They were popping like bacon grease from the frying pan.

"Are you all right?" Rudy said.

"Do I look like I'm all right?"

"No!"

"Well, it figures! They have enough bandages on me to bury an Egyptian pharaoh. I only have a couple of scratches. But they want to haul me into the operating room, for heaven's sake!"

"Here? But why here, Aunt Gussie?"

"I told those ambulance drivers if Cook County was good enough for Quintonia, it was good enough for me." She grunted. "I was wrong there. I want Dr. Kennedy to come in here and make them discharge us both and take us home. Bridget could give me better care than this."

"Bridget's already here," Rudy said.

Aunt Gussie jerked her head toward him, and he saw her eyes go dark with pain.

"You aren't all right," he said. "You got more than a scratch, Aunt Gussie."

"Never mind that! Why is Bridget here?"

Rudy told her about Kenneth. Aunt Gussie closed her eyes, and when she opened them they were misty. "I suppose I should have listened to your father after all," she said. "I only made everything worse by holding that rally. He was right about the mob—only we still don't have what we need to prove it."

"Maybe we do," Rudy said.

Just then, a pair of double doors swung open down the hall. A tall man in a white coat and white cap, followed by a trio of nurses, approached. Rudy was sure he'd seen that fellow somewhere before, and hadn't liked it.

"All right, Mrs. Nitz," the man said. "It's time. We're going to take you in and give you some ether to put you to sleep."

"You are going to do nothing of the sort! I refuse to allow you to lay a hand on me!"

"Common reaction after a gunshot wound," the man said to the nurses. "Now, Mrs. Nitz, if you'll just lie back—" He leaned over, and his cap fell off. His head was completely bald.

"Don't let him operate on you!" Rudy cried.

"Go call Dr. Kennedy!" Aunt Gussie said. "Make him come here—now!"

Rudy gave a panicked nod and headed for the stairs. How he was going to get to Dr. Kennedy's office he didn't have a clue. All he knew was that he had to get the doctor back here somehow. He dug into his pocket, but it was empty. They'd spent all the change on the cab. That meant no bus fare. How did a person get from here to—what street was Dr. Kennedy on?

Nearly in tears again, Rudy jumped over the last four steps and rounded the corner into the waiting room.

"Hey, there you are, kid! You're coming with me!"

The voice came out of nowhere, and went right up Rudy's

backbone. Trying not to knock over any of the tottering, frail people in the hallway, Rudy ran for the front door.

He was almost there when he felt the hand grab the back of his sweater. His feet went off the floor, and he was dangling in the air.

Chapter Sixteen

*J*ust stick with me, kid," said a low, soft voice. "I'm going to carry you right out of here."

Rudy almost wilted in relief. It was Clyde, and he was carrying him toward the front door.

"Sorry, sir," Clyde said over his shoulder to Grunting Man, who watched with narrowed eyes. "He won't bother you anymore. I been lookin' for him all day."

"See he doesn't show his face around here again!" Grunting Man shouted.

"Oh, keep your voice down, Clarence," said the nurse at the desk. "I've had it with that whole Hutchinson crowd!"

The door shut behind them, and Clyde put Rudy down. "Where to, kid?" he said. "I told LaDonna I'd look after you."

"I have to find Dr. Kennedy!" Rudy said.

"Where's his office?"

"I don't remember! I've only been there a couple of times."

"Then why don't we go to your house and call him?" Clyde said.

So Rudy finally got a ride in the Stutz Bearcat. He was too busy asking questions to enjoy it, though.

"How's Kenneth?"

163

"He's still holding his own."

"What about Bridget?"

"She's still holding out for someone who's heard of whatever disease it is Kenneth has."

"Do you know where Little Al went?"

"Nope. Sorry."

Rudy was out of the car almost before Clyde rolled the Bearcat to a stop in front of the house.

"Thanks!" Rudy called back as he took the front steps in one leap. He left the front door swinging open as he burst into the house and headed for the library. But before he could get to the phone, he stopped dead at the sight of Hildy Helen.

She was pacing like a caged animal. The only real caged animal in the room was muttering to himself on his perch, "Where is everybody? Why did they all go off and leave me?"

"Oh," Rudy said.

Hildy Helen looked up from her path on the carpet. Rudy waited for a barrage of scolding and insults, but his sister's face crumpled when she saw him.

"Rudy!" she cried. "I thought you were dead or something!" She drew her hands together under her chin, and Rudy saw that her eyes were red and puffy.

"You've been crying," he said.

"Of course I've been crying! Nobody was here when we got home from school. I thought you'd run away. Then suddenly Little Al wasn't here—you know how he can disappear so fast. And then I went out to look for him a little and when I came back, LaDonna was just pulling away with Clyde—and I've waited and waited and waited." She swiped at her running nose with the back of her hand. "Why does everybody hate me, Rudy?"

Rudy was so confused he couldn't have answered even if he *hadn't* had something else he had to do.

"I gotta call Dr. Kennedy," he said. He went straight for the phone and talked to the operator and waited with his heart throbbing in his throat.

"What's going on, Rudy?" Hildy Helen said. "Why won't anybody tell me?"

"Just a minute," Rudy said. "Hello, this is Rudy Hutchinson."

For about the hundredth time that day, Rudy talked to a nurse. But this one listened, and she put Dr. Kennedy on the line, and after a few sentences from Rudy, he was on his way to Cook County Hospital.

"They're going to operate on Aunt Gussie?" Hildy Helen cried when Rudy hung up the phone.

"No," Rudy replied.

"But you just said—"

"I know, but—"

"Why won't you even tell me anything, Rudy?"

Rudy stared at her. "Why won't *I* tell *you* anything? What are you talking about? You're the one who stopped speaking to me!"

"Well, what do you expect? You were so selfish and made us look stupid in front of all our relatives—"

"So that means I'm not part of the family anymore?" Rudy asked. "You even turned my friends against me!"

"You turned against *me*, Rudy Hutchinson! You took up with LaDonna and did everything with her instead of us! And she was so hateful to us at first!"

"I did that because you wouldn't do anything with me!"

"I didn't know how!"

That one baffled Rudy. "What do you mean, you didn't know how? What's to know? We just—do things."

Hildy Helen shook her head. The tears were dribbling down her cheeks and onto her chin and making big, dark splotches on the front of her dress.

"No," she said, "I didn't know how to ask you after I saw how stupid I was being—and then you seemed to like LaDonna better than me so I had to keep Little Al for myself. I—I—I told him you were only going to get him in trouble. He didn't believe me—he really didn't, Rudy—but he's just so scared of going to prison. You have to believe me! I'm sorry!"

Before Rudy could answer—though what he would have said, he didn't know—Hildy Helen flew past him and out of the library and across the front hall to the stairs.

"Wait, Hildy Helen!" Rudy said.

"No—I hate myself!" she cried.

He followed her out into the hall, and she was already halfway up the first set of steps.

"Just wait!" he said.

She turned to look at him over her shoulder, tripped on the next step, and dropped to the stair carpet like a sack of flour. She put her face in her hands and sobbed.

"Oh, for crying out loud, Hildy Helen, don't keep cryin'," Rudy said.

But she did anyway, and he went slowly toward her and sat on the step next to her.

"Come on, stop it," Rudy said. "I was stupid, too. I never learn from the past—I keep doing the same stupid things over and over."

"But I like your stupid things!" Hildy Helen said. "I just want to do them with you! I wanted to go up in the airplane with you—only you didn't ask me!"

"You said you were scared!"

"But I'd have gone if you did. I always want to do what you do, Rudy!"

That brought on a new onslaught of tears. This time, she threw her face into his lap, and this time, there was no consoling her.

Rudy sat there awkwardly until she stopped crying, and then he tried to shift his legs so she'd get up. It was good to have it all in the open now—it was good to know it was going to be all right with them—but why did girls always have to touch you? Between LaDonna with her forehead-kissing and Hildy Helen with her neck-hugging and now her face in his lap . . .

But her head didn't move even when he did, and when Rudy leaned over, he saw that she was fast asleep. She didn't look any too comfortable either, with her neck all bent like that.

Rudy sighed and pulled his sweater off over his head. It would make a good pillow—

But as he did, three pamphlets fell out and tumbled softly to the next step. Rudy's heart started to pound again.

The communist booklets! He'd forgotten all about those. He stared at them, and his thoughts raced in his head.

Do I give them to Dad and tell him I found them in his office? Or give them to Aunt Gussie and tell her *I found them in Dad's office?*

The lump regrouped in Rudy's throat. Why *did* Dad and Aunt Gussie have these booklets, anyway? Just to study them, maybe, since they were against communism, or since Aunt Gussie had been accused? And why had the booklets been in such out-of-place spots in Dad's office?

Could Bridget have put them there? No, she hadn't worked there since Kenneth had come.

Who? Why? The questions battered at Rudy. There weren't many answers—just one.

I think I have to get rid of these, he decided. *I'll just throw them away and pretend they never existed, and then I won't have to know.*

But he knew right away he couldn't just toss them into the wastepaper basket. They had Aunt Gussie's name in them.

I'll have to burn them, he thought. *Just get rid of every trace, and then everything will be all right.*

He frowned at the booklets, wishing he could burn them right away. *I hate things like this*, he thought. *I hate it when people hate and are stupid and lie and make scenes! I just want to be happy! Is that too much to ask, Jesus? I just want to be happy again.*

Feeling as tired as Hildy Helen had looked, he tucked the pamphlets under the stair carpet for safekeeping until he had a chance to burn them. He leaned his head against the banister and was soon fast asleep.

He was awakened later by a rush of voices from the front doorway. He recognized Aunt Gussie's right off.

"If you do not put me down at once, young man, I shall be forced to whack you with my walking stick."

"Stop your bellyachin', Gussie," Rudy heard Dr. Kennedy say. "I'd have left you back there at the hospital if I'd known you were going to be this much trouble!"

The party appeared in the front hall then, and Rudy felt a laugh bubbling up inside him. There was Aunt Gussie, minus most of her bandages, being carried through by LaDonna's Clyde. Dr. Kennedy followed, smoking one of his cigars and casually swinging his doctor bag.

Rudy stood up, forgetting Hildy Helen in his lap and nearly tumbling her down the stairs.

"Ouch!" she said sleepily, rubbing her neck. When she saw the group, though, she squealed and ran to them. Quintonia took her in her arms.

"You're all right!" Hildy Helen cried.

"No thanks to them hospital people, I'll tell you that," Quintonia said. "I wouldn't let them touch me, no, sir—not till Dr. Kennedy come in and stitched me up himself."

"What happened?" Rudy said.

"Just caught some splinters and such that come flyin' out when that dynamite went off," Quintonia said.

"She's a little shaken up," Dr. Kennedy said. "I'm about to give them both a tranquilizer."

"I do not need a tranquilizer!" Aunt Gussie protested as Clyde deposited her on the sofa where Kenneth had spent so much time lately.

"Neither do I!" said Quintonia.

"Well, *we* need for you to have them," Dr. Kennedy said. "Don't we?"

LaDonna and Clyde both nodded emphatically. Hildy Helen couldn't stop hugging Quintonia. Rudy made a beeline for Little Al.

"Where did you disappear to?" Rudy said. "Every time I turn around, you come up missing."

"I was in a closet," Little Al said. His face was smug and shining. "Same one I pushed Miss Gussie's cart into when that baldy doctor went into the operating room and those nurses tried to wheel her in there." He grinned. "I give 'em a run for their money, and then I stashed Miss Gustavio in the closet."

Dr. Kennedy chuckled. "Alonzo greeted me at the front door of Cook County with, 'Hurry up, Doc, I got Miss Gustavio in a closet.'" He knocked his cigar ash into the Grecian water jar next to the sofa. "I never know what I'm going to run into with the Hutchinsons."

"Did you dig out her bullet right there in the closet?" Rudy asked.

"What bullet?" Dr. Kennedy said. "She had a flesh wound, which I am about to dress right here and now."

LaDonna came over to the couch. "I know you've done so much already, Doctor, but could you tell me—"

"About your little brother?" Dr. Kennedy stuck the whole cigar into the water jar and shook his head. "Sad case, sad case. If that young redhead hadn't caught his symptoms, he might be dead right here on this couch."

"Harry, really!" Aunt Gussie said.

"He was too sick to come home with us," Dr. Kennedy said. "But the only reason I left him there was because he had his private nurse."

"Bridget isn't a nurse," Aunt Gussie said. "She's my personal secretary."

"Well, that's a waste of her talents," Dr. Kennedy said. "She ought to be a nurse. She'd make a darn fine one." He began unwrapping the bandage on Aunt Gussie's arm. "I think she ought to go with him to New York."

"New York!" LaDonna said.

"Quintonia, Harry, and I discussed it on the way home," Aunt Gussie said, "but I did intend to talk to you about it first, of course." She glared at Dr. Kennedy, who continued blithely unwrapping her wound. "There is a very fine clinic in New York where they are treating people with sickle-cell anemia. I will pay for his treatment if you and Quintonia will agree to let him go."

"Will it mean saving his life?" LaDonna said.

"It's about the only chance he has," Dr. Kennedy said.

"And it's a very good chance," Aunt Gussie said, still glaring at him, "because we will all be praying. The Hutchinsons have always—"

"Have always prayed," Dr. Kennedy finished for her. "Yes, I know. And it's a good thing. Look at that arm! Barely a scratch. You should have been killed out there, Gussie—or at least maimed for life."

"Thank you, Harry," she said dryly. "Now—"

"Aunt Gussie?" Hildy Helen said suddenly. "Where is Dad?"

"Now that is the question, isn't it?" Aunt Gussie said. "We are all accounted for except your father and Sol." She looked a little shame-faced. "I told Sol to drive your father today, that we didn't need him. Then Quintonia and I slipped off to Haymarket Square on the bus."

Little Al grinned. "Have I ever told you I like an old doll like you, Miss Gustavio?"

There was a knock at the door, and Hildy Helen jumped up. "Let me get it," she said. "I haven't gotten to do anything to help today."

She returned white-faced, followed by three men in police uniforms. One of them was a very solemn Officer O'Dell.

"My favorite copper!" Little Al said to him.

Al stepped up to the tall policeman to shake his hand. Officer O'Dell returned his handshake, but didn't give his usual smile.

"This isn't a social call, I'm afraid, Al," he said. He took off his hat and nodded at Aunt Gussie. "I'm very sorry, Mrs. Nitz."

Rudy's stomach began to churn.

"Sorry for what?" Aunt Gussie said. "Gentlemen, to what do we owe the honor of your presence?"

"No need for none of that fancy talk," said one of the other officers, who looked just like his fellow policeman as far as Rudy could tell. "Like we told your chauffeur—"

"Sol?" Aunt Gussie said. She shook Dr. Kennedy off her arm and sat up on the sofa. "Where is Sol?"

"He's at the station with your nephew. We're asking them both a couple of questions."

"I do not approve of this, Mrs. Nitz," Officer O'Dell said. "But please cooperate with them so we can get this embarrassment over with and everyone can get back to their lives."

"What embarrassment?" Aunt Gussie asked impatiently. "What is all this about?"

Rudy looked around the room. Everyone's face was stretched and bewildered. His own cheeks were already on fire.

"We've come to search your residence," Officer Number One said. "We have orders. Here they are."

"Search it for what?"

"Evidence."

"Well, no kidding!" LaDonna burst out. "Evidence of what?"

Both officers looked at her in momentary surprise, then turned back to Aunt Gussie as if LaDonna were invisible.

"We have reason to believe that you yourself incited today's riot," said Officer Number Two.

"You are, after all, a suspected communist," Number One put in.

"We have already searched your nephew's office," said Number Two. "He comes up clean so far. Now we search your home. Shall we get to it?"

"I shall not," Officer O'Dell told him icily. "I came because I was ordered to, but I refuse to participate in this. I'm here to protect Mrs. Nitz and her family."

"Suit yourself," said one of them. He turned to the other. "You start in the front room," he said. "I'll take this room. If you folks wouldn't mind stepping into the hallway—"

"We would indeed!" Dr. Kennedy said. "I have injured people here!"

"I can't help that," came the reply. "Carry 'em out if you need to—I don't care. But somebody's gotta keep an eye on 'em."

Clyde once more scooped Aunt Gussie up and carried her out, while Little Al and Hildy Helen helped Quintonia limp her way into the hall.

"They better not mess up my kitchen," Rudy heard her say. Her voice was full of tears.

Rudy wasn't much different. He was sure he was about to be sick.

What should I do? he thought.

If Aunt Gussie is innocent and they find those pamphlets under the stair carpet, what then?

But if she's really guilty and they find them—

Rudy shook himself. *What am I thinking? Aunt Gussie can't*

*be guilty. She's a Hutchinson! She prays. She believes in Jesus.
She stands for what's right.*

I know that from—from the past.

He'd learned that much from history, anyway.

Rudy slipped past Dr. Kennedy and LaDonna and got to Aunt
Gussie, in the chair where Clyde had placed her like a queen. She
was watching the officer with imperious eyes as he opened her
mummy case and picked up ancient vases to stare inside them.

"Those are priceless artifacts!" she was saying. "If you break
them, they can't be replaced."

"Aunt Gussie?" Rudy whispered.

"What is it, Rudolph? Not now—"

But she seemed to catch herself, and she looked up at Rudy.
He got down on one knee and put his lips close to her ear. "I want
to tell you something," he whispered.

She nodded. She kept her eyes on the officer, but Rudy could
tell she was listening.

In whispered spurts he told her what he'd found and how he'd
stuffed the pamphlets under his sweater.

"And right now," he murmured, "they're under the stair carpet."

"Check under the stair carpet!" a voice barked.

Rudy spasmed up from the floor. There was Officer Number—
Whatever—standing in the doorway from the parlor, smiling ma-
liciously.

"It pays to keep your ears open," he said to Rudy.

Rudy sank back to the floor as the other officer marched im-
portantly to the stairs and lifted the carpet. The first few steps
revealed nothing. The fourth one gave up three pamphlets.

"The Communist Manifesto in America," the policeman said.
"Well, well, well."

"Open it. Does it have her name in it?" said the other one.

He opened it, then smiled as if he'd just found the toy in the Cracker Jacks.

" 'This Book Belongs to Gustavia Nitz,' " he said.

"Then I guess, Mrs. Nitz, that's right where you put them." He turned to Officer O'Dell, whose weathered face bore a look of pain. "Since you're such good friends with Mrs. Nitz, Officer O'Dell, why don't you do the honors?" He tossed a pair of hand-cuffs, which rattled as they landed in Officer O'Dell's hands.

"I'm so sorry about this," O'Dell said to Aunt Gussie as he came toward her. "I'll try not to make this uncomfortable."

He snapped open the cuffs. Aunt Gussie offered her wrists.

Rudy couldn't stand it.

"No!" he shouted. "She didn't put them there! I did!"

Chapter Seventeen

T here was a moment of stunned silence. Rudy kept his eyes on Officer Number One. He watched the policeman's face lose its confused look and try to appear shocked.

"Now doesn't that just take the cake?" he said. "Bringin' a young kid into it like that! It's shameful."

The other officer shook his head as he moved toward Rudy. "Poor kid doesn't even know what he's doin'."

Rudy heard a click. He looked down to see the officer unclasping another pair of handcuffs.

"Hey, whatta ya doin'?" Little Al cried. "You ain't cuffin' Rudolpho! He ain't done nothin'!"

"I have to disagree with ya, kid," the officer said. The cuffs were poised above Rudy's wrist. Aunt Gussie stuck out a still-free hand and snatched them away.

"For heaven's sake, be reasonable!" she said. "Listen to the boy. We've all stopped doing that, and it's ridiculous. Listen to him!"

"Do it," Officer O'Dell said. "It's the least we can do."

Both officers looked disgruntled, but Number One nodded. "Go ahead, kid. You got two minutes."

"Take all the time you need, Rudy," Officer O'Dell said.

Rudy swallowed hard and looked up at Aunt Gussie. She was watching him carefully. Her eyes were trusting. Her head was nodding. He swallowed again, and the lump went down, and he began.

"First thing I want to say is that I saw who threw the dynamite at the rally—and it sure wasn't Aunt Gussie."

"How would you know, kid?"

"Because I was there—up on the fire escape on the corner of Randolph and DesPlaines. I saw three different men leaning out windows, and I saw them all throw bunches of dynamite."

Officer O'Dell drew himself up tall. "Some of the people on the scene reported hearing someone call out a warning just before the explosion."

"That was you, kid?" said Number One. "How convenient."

"So," the other one said, parking his thumbs in his belt, "you'd identify these men—even if they turned out to be mobsters?"

Rudy didn't hesitate. "Yes, sir, I would."

They both grunted as if they were one person. "We'll see about that when the time comes," Number Two said.

"You sure will!" Little Al said. "Rudy'll do it. I know that for a fact."

"I'm so glad we got all these kids telling us how to do our job, aren't you?" Two said to One.

"Rudy is a reliable witness," Officer O'Dell said. "I know this family. Known 'em for years."

"Yeah, that's all well and good," Number One said, "but that still doesn't tell us what we really want to know."

"Yeah, and that's how you got those pamphlets in the first place."

"I brought them here so I could burn them," Rudy said quickly.

"You were going to destroy evidence? Oh, now there's a reliable witness!"

"Because I knew they didn't belong to Aunt Gussie!"

"But where did you get them? Where'd you find them, kid?"

Rudy couldn't answer. He couldn't get the next words to come out of his mouth.

"Look, kid. You either tell us the whole story, or we don't buy any of it, you got that?"

Rudy looked around wildly for someone to save him from having to answer.

"Go on, Rudy," LaDonna said softly. "Tell the truth. It'll be all right."

"It's always all right when you tell the truth," Aunt Gussie said. "You're a Hutchinson. You stand for right. Tell the man where you found them."

Rudy took a deep breath and closed his eyes so he wouldn't have to look at the policemen. "I found them in my father's office," he said.

"Well, there you have it, don't you?" said one of the policemen. "Her nephew is the communist!"

"I refuse to believe that, just as I refuse to arrest this good woman!" Officer O'Dell said. "If it's to be done, you do it. I don't want it on my head."

"Don't be a fool, O'Dell," said Number One. "If Hutchinson isn't guilty, how did this pinko reading material get into his office? That's what I wanna know."

"I know!"

They all looked at Little Al, who was suddenly in the middle of the hall, eyes flashing. "Rudolpho!" he said. "It was that delivery boy! Remember—the one was comin' out of Mr. Hutchie's office when we went in? I thought he looked too old to be a delivery boy!"

"Beautiful," said Number Two, "now I got two brats screamin' that they're witnesses."

"Reliable witnesses," Office O'Dell said again. "The only decent thing to do is take the whole group down to the station and sort it out down there. Detective Zorn needs to hear this."

They were on their way, tucked into the back seat of a police car, before Rudy could get himself to speak again. It seemed everything he said only brought more trouble.

"I'm sorry, Aunt Gussie," he said to her.

"For what? For telling the truth? For standing up for me?"

"Cut the chatter back there, the both of ya," Officer Number One said from the front seat.

"I wish we coulda ridden with Officer O'Dell," Rudy whispered.

Aunt Gussie nodded. Then she reached over and put her hand on top of Rudy's. He let her keep it there.

When they reached the station, Rudy was afraid he would see his father sitting on the other side of a set of bars. But Dad wasn't in a cell. He was sitting in Detective Zorn's office, pacing up and down while the detective watched him from his desk. Rudy was glad to see that. Dad trusted Detective Zorn.

Seeing Aunt Gussie and Rudy and Little Al walk in, Dad came across the room and put his arms around all three of them at once.

"I'm sorry, Dad," was all Rudy could think of to say.

"I'm not! You're all safe, alive, not hurt." He glanced at Aunt Gussie's arm. "What happened here?"

"It's what happens when you don't listen to wise counsel," she said. "But then, we've all made that mistake, haven't we?"

She looked at Rudy and gave him a hint of smile.

"I've been in here all day trying to convince these people that you and I are not communist conspirators and that we didn't start that riot in the Haymarket."

"I know I've put you in a difficult position, James, by even being there. I thought I had to go and speak."

"Thanks to Detective Zorn, they haven't locked me up yet."

"Well, they were about to lock *me* up when Rudolph came to the rescue. How about those photos you want him to identify?" she said to Officer Number One.

"What photos?" Detective Zorn said.

The two policemen looked at each other. They didn't seem as smug now as they had at the house. In fact, Rudy thought they looked a little worried. Finally they took turns mumbling to the detective about Rudy's story—the men throwing the dynamite and the delivery boy coming out of Dad's office.

Dad gave a grunt when they were finished. "Are you two the very same police officers who were in here grilling me all afternoon?" he said.

"You know we are. What kind of question is that?"

"I just had to make sure. You certainly have a different attitude than you did earlier. Do you see it, Detective?"

Detective Zorn nodded.

"I think it's fear I see in your eyes now," Dad said.

"Fear!"

"Fear, that's it." Dad's eyes narrowed behind his glasses. "You're afraid now because you know it was the mob, even without Rudy looking at your photos. Now you can't pin it on my aunt or even my son."

"I think making you the scapegoat was what Al Capone had in mind, Mr. Hutchinson." It was Officer O'Dell, standing tall and quiet in the doorway. "I think he had his boys out to get you."

O'Dell swept the room with his eyes, then turned and left. Both officers stomped out after him, smoke practically coming out of their ears.

"You know our orders from the chief," Rudy heard one of them say.

Detective Zorn shut the door behind them. "Let's have a look at those mug shots, boys," he said.

Presented with a photo album full of menacing faces, Rudy didn't take long to find the three men he had seen in the windows. He was surprised to find another familiar face in there, too.

"This one was the delivery boy," he said.

Little Al looked over Rudy's shoulder. "That's him, all right. What delivery boy has a mustache, now I ask you?"

Detective Zorn snapped the book closed. "I've had enough of looking at those faces," he said. "You're all free to go. You may be called on to testify in court, though I doubt it."

"Why not?" Little Al said. "I'd like to be on the good side in court for once!"

"Because those were Capone's men you pointed out," Detective Zorn said. "I'll issue warrants for their arrest, and they might be brought in, but it will never stick. Mind you, I'll try, but Capone will get them out of it somehow."

"But people were badly hurt!" Aunt Gussie said. "One young woman was killed! You're going to let this drop—just because you're afraid of the mob?"

"There isn't much I can do alone," Detective Zorn said. "Not when our own chief is under the outfit's thumb."

"Keep trying," Dad said. "You know *I* will."

"I will," Detective Zorn said. "But I can't move mountains." He managed a half smile. "After all, I'm not a Hutchinson."

They all took turns shaking the detective's hand. Then, quietly, they walked down the hall and onto the street.

"At least we're not arrested," Rudy told Aunt Gussie. He rubbed his wrists. "I didn't like the looks of those handcuffs."

"But we've gotten absolutely nowhere," Aunt Gussie said. Her voice was hard with disgust. "We all tried, and we all prayed. But as long as Capone is allowed to be in power, it's hard to get anything right accomplished."

"Except for one thing," Dad said. "One very important thing."

"What's that?"

"I've gotten my faith back."

"Why, James! I didn't know you'd lost faith in the Lord!"

"No, not that faith, Auntie," Dad said. Then, to Rudy's surprise, he put out his hand and touched Rudy's shoulder. "I mean, I've gotten back my faith in my son. I was too hard on you, Rudy. And as usual, I got too wrapped up in my own business and didn't pay enough attention to you. You think I'd learn from the past."

Rudy felt himself grin. "It's hard, Dad," he said. "It's hard."

"You know what's harder'n that?" Little Al said.

"Oh, do tell, Alonzo," Aunt Gussie said.

Little Al nodded down the street. "Gettin' picked up in front of the police station in a pink car."

"I don't care what color it is," Dad said as Sol pulled up to the curb. "Let's go home."

Chapter Eighteen

*T*wo weeks later, spring had turned to summer in Chicago. Quintonia claimed you could fry an egg on the sidewalk, though she was quick to warn Little Al and Hildy Helen and Rudy not to try it.

They were contemplating that on a steamy Saturday evening as they sat on the front steps waiting for Clyde to pick up La-Donna for the prom. Of course, fried eggs and LaDonna's pink gown weren't the only topics of conversation. Mostly they were discussing their upcoming sixth grade graduation.

"Miss Tibbs says we're going to wear all white and walk across the stage to get our diplomas," Hildy Helen said. "I wish Bridget were still here to go shopping with me."

"I miss that doll already," Little Al said.

Rudy felt the same way, and he kind of missed Kenneth, too. It had only been a few days since they'd left for New York—Kenneth to check into the special hospital, Bridget to take care of him and go to nursing school. At first Bridget had protested about Aunt Gussie paying for her classes, but Aunt Gussie said she'd rather spend her money on Bridget's education than on shoes to match LaDonna's prom gown. Of course, she'd bought those, too, and three longs strands of pearls and silk hose.

LaDonna just had to promise not to wear them rolled below her knees.

"You two will look smashing in white suits," Hildy Helen went on.

"Do we have to talk about clothes?" Rudy said.

"Do we have to talk about graduation?" Little Al said. "I don't even know if I'm gonna pass."

"But you passed all your examinations," Hildy Helen said. "You even got a high grade in history."

"Yeah, thanks to Rudolpho."

"What did I do?" Rudy said. He shrugged uncomfortably. It was one of the many things he still felt guilty about.

"You showed me it wasn't so bad learnin' about all that stuff that happened in the past," Little Al said.

"How'd I do that?"

"When we was back in Virginia, I seen how proud you was of bein' a Hutchinson, so I figured I oughta be, too, and learn about 'em." Little Al frowned down at his hands. "But you heard Miss Tibbs yourself. She said that night she couldn't pass me."

"Maybe she changed her mind," Hildy Helen said stubbornly.

"Why don't you ask her?" Rudy said. He pointed to the corner where a bus was just pulling away, and Miss Tibbs was crossing the street toward the house.

"She hasn't been here in a long time," Hildy Helen said. "I was starting to think maybe she and Dad weren't stuck on each other anymore."

She got up and ran to escort Miss Tibbs across the lawn. Rudy looked anxiously at Little Al. His brother was carefully studying the palms of his hands.

What if he doesn't graduate with us? Rudy thought. *He's right. She said she couldn't pass him—not in good conscience. Why didn't I straighten up sooner? Things might've been different.*

"I see some awfully long faces here," Miss Tibbs said.

Both boys looked up at her, but neither of them smiled.

"Oh, my," she said. "More trouble for your family? You've had so much lately. And I've been so wrapped up with my own that I haven't been much help."

Her voice trailed off, and she watched them. Nobody could say anything. Finally, Little Al tried to lean casually against the steps and said, "Nothin' new, Miss Dollface. Just the same old thing—I'm dumb."

To Rudy's surprise, Miss 'Dollface' threw her sandy head back and laughed—a big, old belly laugh. "Al, you are anything but dumb!" she said. "Whatever in the world gave you that idea?"

"Well, you did, Miss Dollface," Little Al said.

Miss Tibbs looked at him blankly. Then she looked at Rudy and Hildy Helen. They both nodded solemnly.

"What on earth are you three talking about?" she said. "When did I ever say Al was anything but bright?"

"You didn't exactly say that," Hildy Helen said.

"We were listening in when we shouldn't have been," Rudy said. He was trying to own up to all his mistakes these days, hoping maybe some of them would disappear for good. There were still so many hanging over his head.

"And you heard what, exactly?" Miss Tibbs said. Her fair brow was furrowed into tiny lines.

"You said you couldn't pass me, not in good conscious," Little Al said.

"Conscience," Hildy Helen said.

For a moment Miss Tibbs looked befuddled. Then slowly her forehead came unwrinkled, and she began to shake her head. "That will teach you three to eavesdrop," she said. "I wasn't talking about Little Al. I was talking about—someone else."

"Who?" they all said.

Then one by one they clapped their hands over their mouths,

and Miss Tibbs laughed again. "It doesn't matter. I have to pass him anyway. The boy's father has seen to that."

"Somebody givin' you the business, Miss Dollface?" Little Al demanded.

Miss Tibbs smiled and patted his knee. "I'm getting over it." She turned to Rudy. "I owe you an apology, Rudy. I was hard on you that day you asked me about Little Al. I understand now what you were getting at. I misjudged you, and I shouldn't have. Forgive me?"

Rudy shrugged. "Sure," he said. He could feel his face coloring, but it wasn't a bad kind of embarrassed. Still, he was glad when Miss Tibbs got up and started into the house.

"Oh, and Al," she said, stopping by the door. "I won't keep you in suspense any longer. Of course you're going to graduate. You are ready for junior high in every way I can think of. You keep following Rudy's lead, and you'll be fine."

When she was gone, Little Al punched Rudy on the arm. "It's you and me, Rudolpho. Only you're gonna have to follow my lead when it comes to some stuff."

"Like what?" Rudy said.

"Like—this stuff!"

He grabbed Rudy around the head with his arm and dragged him to the ground.

"Lemme go, Al!"

"Not till you holler uncle!"

"Boys!"

"Lay off, Hildy Helen. This is boy business," Al said.

"No, really—stop."

"Why?"

"Because some people are coming, and I don't know them."

"Who are they, gangsters?" Rudy asked with a laugh. "I thought we knew all the gangsters!" He was still laughing when he pulled his head out of Little Al's armpit, but his smile faded when he saw what Hildy Helen was talking about.

Three boys in dashing white dinner jackets with red carnations in their lapels were climbing out of a Model T. Their faces were grim, and their shoulders had a determined swagger as they crossed toward the children. Hildy Helen moved closer to Rudy.

Little Al took on a swagger of his own, even sitting still. "What can we do for ya?" he said, giving them a charmer smile.

One of them, a blond boy with his hair parted slightly off center, looked doubtfully up at Aunt Gussie's mansion. "This isn't where LaDonna Hutchinson lives, is it?" he said.

"Sure is," Little Al said.

A second boy, whose freckles covered even his hands, smirked. "What is she, your maid or something?"

"She's our maid's niece," Rudy said. He felt his cheeks burning. *Why did I say that?* he thought. *LaDonna is family*.

"Actually, she's like our cousin," he said.

The three boys laughed all at once, as if they were sharing the same voice box.

"So, what do you want with her?" Rudy said.

"We don't want anything with her," the blond one said. "That's why we're here."

"Yeah," said the one with the freckles. "Maybe you kids could deliver a message for us."

"Like what?" Rudy said. He could feel his eyes squinting behind his glasses.

"Like . . . this is her last warning. We've tried to tell her not to come to the prom or she'll be sorry."

"What do you mean, her last warning?" Rudy said. He stood up on the step, nearly knocking Hildy Helen over in the process.

"Just what I said," answered the blond kid. "We've told her three times. She and her spade boyfriend don't show up or—"

"Don't call them spades," Rudy said. "We don't allow that kind of talk around here."

The freckled one snorted. "Oh, yes, *sir!*" he said.

He executed an elaborate salute, but Rudy wasn't swayed. "I think you're lying," he said. "I don't think you ever warned her or she would have told us."

"I think she didn't tell you," growled the freckled kid, "because she knew your old man wouldn't let her go. He wouldn't let her embarrass him in front of the whole neighborhood when we run her and what's-his-name out of there."

"His name is Clyde," Rudy said. "And he's just as good as you—no, he's better. And so is LaDonna. She's going to the prom no matter what you say, and there better not be any trouble, or my old man will do worse than embarrass you, you can believe that."

The third one, the one with the protruding front teeth, shrank back and laughed. "I'm scared. How about you fellas?"

"I *would* be afraid if I were you," said a voice behind Rudy.

The three boys' eyes flipped to the door. Rudy didn't have to turn around to know Dad was standing there.

"My son is right," Dad said. "It's against the law for anyone to bar Negroes who attend a school from participating in any of that school's activities. So, if you make trouble for LaDonna and Clyde or any of their other Negro friends, I will have you hauled into court. It's very simple."

Freckles and Buck Teeth could only stare, open-mouthed. Blondie managed a smirk.

"My old man's a big man in this city," he said. "He's powerful. He has money."

"Oh, spare me," Dad said. His voice was weary as he ran his hand through his wavy dark hair. "Believe me, I've come up against tougher and more powerful and richer men than he is. Unless, of course, your father is a gangster."

"My old man? No!"

"Tell him not to cross me, then," Dad said. "I'm sick and tired of rich, powerful people taking advantage of those who don't have the means to fight for themselves. And when I get tired, I get cranky. Listen to my son. For every embarrassing moment you might cause LaDonna, I will embarrass you tenfold."

Dad said nothing more, and neither did anyone else. The three boys backed away from the front steps and hurried off to their Model T. Their heads were bent together as if they were making some sort of plan, but Dad chuckled to himself.

"They're saving face," he said. "I don't think we'll have any more trouble from them. Just in case, though . . ."

"Mister Jim, sir?" said a soft voice from behind him.

Rudy looked back to see something pink filling up the doorway with its glow. Dad stepped out of the way, and Rudy had to swallow hard.

It was LaDonna, frothed in pink and lace from head to toe, yet outshining every inch of her costume with the smile on her face.

She's prettier than Mary Pickford, he decided. *Prettier than any movie star.*

Dad put out his arm and LaDonna grasped it. She took the steps daintily and stopped when she got to Rudy. Rudy had the urge to run. She was doubtless going to kiss him on the forehead in front of everybody, and he knew he wouldn't be able to keep his face from turning red.

But it didn't feel red yet—not even after all that yelling at those three ridiculous boys in their dinner jackets, and not even after "making a scene." He wasn't embarrassed at all.

"Thank you, Rudy," LaDonna said. "You've come a long way from that little brat who pulled my stockings down in the middle of Union Station."

Rudy felt his eyes bug out, but LaDonna only smiled at him. "Now I *know* you are going to turn out to be the best Hutchinson of all," she said.

Then, eyes sparkling, she kissed the tip of her index finger and pressed it to his forehead.

Rudy could hear the Stutz Bearcat pulling into the driveway. He could hear Miss Tibbs exclaiming about how handsome Clyde looked. But he couldn't take his eyes off of LaDonna—not until she turned and went to meet Clyde.

"That was so sweet!" Hildy Helen whispered to Rudy.

"What was?" Rudy said.

"The way she thanked you and gave you a kiss with her fingertip! It was so—romantic!"

"It was not either!" Rudy said. "Yuck!"

Hildy Helen rolled her eyes. "I will never understand boys," she said.

"Thank you for standing up for us, Mr. Hutchinson, you and Rudy," Clyde said in his soft, low voice. "LaDonna just told me."

"I intend to do more than that," Dad said. "I don't expect any trouble from them. But just to be sure you have a wonderful evening, what do you say some bodyguards follow?"

"Uh—bodyguards, sir?"

"Rudy, Hildy Helen, Little Al, myself. I promise we won't come inside the school unless you give us the signal, all right?"

"I think it's more than all right," LaDonna said. "I would be proud to know you all were out there standing behind us."

Clyde nodded. "But, Mr. Hutchinson, sir, do you have to come in that—pink thing?" He tilted his head toward the Pierce Arrow.

It was in the pink thing that they did go. Rudy sat up front with Dad while Little Al and Hildy Helen watched from the back seat.

"I wish I were in there dancing the Charleston and the fox trot," Hildy Helen said wistfully.

"No need to rush growing up, my dear," Dad said. "You've all done so much growing already, just in the past few months, I can hardly keep up."

By ten o'clock, it looked as if there wasn't going to be any trouble at the prom for LaDonna and Clyde. They came out twice to wave from the doorway, and their only signal was their moonlight smiles.

"Shall we head back to Prairie Avenue, then?" Dad said.

There was no answer from the back seat. Both Hildy Helen and Little Al were sound asleep.

Dad didn't start the car. Instead, he smiled and leaned back. "Maybe we should just sit a while, eh, son?"

Rudy nodded.

"I was really proud of you tonight."

"Thanks."

"Yes, sir, I think you really deserve the graduation present Aunt Gussie has planned for you."

"For me?" Rudy said. "What present?"

"A ride in an airplane. A Junkers G24 to be precise. The whole family's going, of course. You wouldn't want it any other way, would you?"

"No, but what about—"

"What about prejudice and discrimination?" Dad said. He smiled. "Aunt Gussie and I have found a pilot who shares our beliefs about justice—a Christian, as a matter of fact. I think you'll like him."

"If he likes Quintonia and LaDonna, I'll like him."

"That's what I like to hear. You know what else I like to hear?"

"What?"

"That other people are learning from you."

"From me? Nah!"

"Oh, yes. Just tonight before we left to come here, Miss Tibbs told me that after listening to you tell those three boys off, she's decided she's going to fight passing Maury Worthington—no matter how much trouble his father makes for her. We'll have to stand behind her, of course."

So it was *Maury, just like we figured,* Rudy thought. Of course, it all made sense now. Maury being so cocky, calling out things in class, bragging to Rudy that he could do just about whatever he wanted.

"And then there's Little Al—trying to straighten up by following you."

"Maybe," Rudy said shyly.

"LaDonna. If it weren't for you, she might have remained the bitter young woman she was when she first came here. You made friends with her, even though she was acting mean as a snake."

"That was mostly because everybody else was mad at me," Rudy said. "We kind of had to stick together."

"Correction," Dad said. "I think God put you together." Dad was quiet for a moment. "You pray a lot, don't you, Rudy?"

"I do now," Rudy said.

"Then you know when you talk to God things eventually work out right. We may not see it happen right away, but He's in there working for us."

"Is that the way you think it is with you and the mob?" Rudy said.

"Right. I know someday, somehow, we'll beat them. I just keep praying and working. That's all we can do, any of us."

They sat for a while in silence. From inside the school, the strains of "Good Night, Ladies" floated out into the soft summer air.

"That's the last dance," Dad said. He stretched and gave Rudy's shoulder a squeeze. "I know you aren't as anxious as Hildy Helen to go to proms and all that, but you do have a bright future ahead of you. The best is yet to come, you know."

Rudy liked that thought. He settled back into the leather seat and pictured things in his mind like a prayer-drawing—the days ahead, going to junior high with Hildy Helen and Little Al, watching LaDonna graduate from high school, seeing Bridget in a nurse's cap and Kenneth running and playing with the rest of them.

He didn't know how much of the picture would come true. But he could pray that it would.

The pink Pierce Arrow pulled smoothly from the curb, heading for Prairie Avenue. Rudy gazed out the window, still picturing the days ahead. But suddenly he found himself wanting to look back, too.

You know something, Jesus? he thought. *I also like what I learn from the past.*

Yeah. He liked that picture, too.

There's More Adventure in the
CHRISTIAN HERITAGE SERIES!

The Salem Years, 1689–1691

The Rescue #1

Josiah Hutchinson's sister Hope is terribly ill. Can a stranger—whose presence could destroy the family's relationship with everyone else in Salem Village—save her?

The Stowaway #2

Josiah's dream of becoming a sailor seems within reach. But will the evil schemes of a tough orphan named Simon land Josiah and his sister in a heap of trouble?

The Guardian #3

Josiah has a plan to deal with the wolves threatening the town. Can he carry it out without endangering himself—or Cousin Rebecca, who'll follow him anywhere?

The Accused #4

Robbed by the cruel Putnam brothers, Josiah suddenly finds himself on trial for crimes he didn't commit. Can he convince anyone of his innocence?

The Samaritan #5

Josiah tries to help a starving widow and her daughter. But will his feud with the Putnams wreck everything he's worked for?

The Secret #6

If Papa finds out who Hope's been sneaking away to see, he'll be furious! Josiah knows her secret; should he tell?

The Williamsburg Years, 1780–1781

The Rebel #1

Josiah's great-grandson, Thomas Hutchinson, didn't rob the apothecary shop where he works. So why does he wind up in jail, and will he ever get out?

The Thief #2

Someone's stealing horses in Williamsburg! But is the masked rider Josiah sees the real culprit, and who's behind the mask?

The Burden #3

Thomas knows secrets he can't share. So what can he do when a crazed Walter Clark holds him at gunpoint over a secret he doesn't even know?

The Prisoner #4

As war rages in Williamsburg, Thomas' mentor refuses to fight and is carried off by the Patriots. Now which side will Thomas choose?

The Invasion #5

Word comes that Benedict Arnold and his men are ransacking plantations. Can Thomas and his family protect their homestead—even when it's invaded by British soldiers who take Caroline as a hostage?

The Battle #6

Thomas is surrounded by war! Can he tackle still another fight, taking orders from a woman he doesn't like—and being forbidden to talk about his missing brother?

The Charleston Years, 1860–1861

The Misfit #1

When the crusade to abolish slavery reaches full swing, Thomas Hutchinson's great-grandson Austin is sent to live with slave-holding relatives. How can he ever fit in?

The Ally #2

Austin resolves to teach young slave Henry-James to read, even though it's illegal. If Uncle Drayton finds out, will both boys pay the ultimate price?

The Threat #3

Trouble follows Austin to Uncle Drayton's vacation home. Who are those two men Austin hears scheming against his uncle—and why is a young man tampering with the family stagecoach?

The Trap #4

Austin's slave friend Henry-James beats hired hand Narvel in a wrestling match. Will Narvel get the revenge he seeks by picking fights and trapping Austin in a water well?

The Hostage #5

As north and south move toward civil war, Austin is kidnapped by men determined to stop his father from preaching against slavery. Can he escape?

The Escape #6

With the Civil War breaking out, Austin tries to keep Uncle Drayton from selling Henry-James at the slave auction. Will it work, and can Austin flee South Carolina with the rest of the Hutchinsons before Confederate soldiers find them?

The Chicago Years, 1928–1929

The Trick #1

Rudy and Hildy Helen Hutchinson and their father move to Chicago to live with their rich great-aunt Gussie. Can they survive the bullies they find—not to mention Little Al, a young schemer with hopes of becoming a mobster?

The Chase #2

Rudy and his family face one problem after another—including an accident that sends Rudy to the doctor, and the disappearance of Little Al. But can they make it through a deadly dispute between the mob and the Ku Klux Klan?

The Capture #3

It's Christmastime, but Rudy finds nothing to celebrate. Will his attorney father's defense of a Jewish boy accused of murder—and Hildy Helen's kidnapping—ruin far more than the holiday?

The Stunt #4

Rudy gets in trouble wing-walking on a plane. But can he stay standing as he finds himself in the middle of a battle for racial equality—and Aunt Gussie's dangerous fight for workers' rights?

Available at a Christian bookstore near you

FOCUS ON THE FAMILY®

Like this book?

Then you'll love *Clubhouse* magazine! It's written for kids just like you, and it's loaded with great stories, interesting articles, puzzles, games, and fun things for you to do. Some issues include posters, too! With your parents' permission, we'll even send you a complimentary copy.

Simply write to Focus on the Family, Colorado Springs, CO 80995 (in Canada, write P.O. 9800, Stn. Terminal, Vancouver, B.C. V6B 4G3) and mention that you saw this offer in the back of this book. Or, call 1-800-A-FAMILY (in Canada, call 1-800-661-9800).

You may also visit our Web site (www.family.org) to learn more about the ministry or find out if there is a Focus on the Family office in your country.

● ● ●

"Adventures in Odyssey" is a fantastic series of books, videos, and radio dramas that's fun for the entire family—parents, too! You'll love the twists and turns found in the novels, as well as the excitement packed into every video. And the 30 albums of radio dramas (available on audiocassette or compact disc) are great to listen to in the car, after dinner . . . even at bedtime! You can hear "Adventures in Odyssey" on the radio, too. Call Focus on the Family for a listing of local stations airing these programs or to request any of the "Adventures in Odyssey" resources. They're also available at Christian bookstores everywhere.

Focus on the Family is an organization that is dedicated to helping you and your family establish lasting, loving relationships with each other and the Lord. It's why we exist! If we can assist you or your family in any way, please feel free to contact us. We'd love to hear from you!